A Peridale Cafe MYSTERY

AGATHA FROST

pink tree
PUBLISHING

For questions and comments about this book, please contact
pinktreepublishing@gmail.com

www.pinktreepublishing.com
www.agathafrost.com

ISBN: 9781790340170
Imprint: Independently published

ALSO BY AGATHA FROST

A Peridale Cafe MYSTERY

Book Fifteen

1

J ulia awoke with a feeling that something was very wrong. Bolting upright, she looked around her bedroom. The pale, November-morning light streamed through her curtains.

Sunlight.

Her grey Maine Coon, Mowgli, was snuggled up where her fiancé, Barker, should have been. She scratched at her head as she let out a yawn; Mowgli did the same. It would have been so easy to fall back and let her fluffy pillows return her to her dreams. She was exhausted, after all, and her room was nice and toasty for once. Was the radiator on?

Radiator heat.

Julia rubbed her eyes as she tried to focus. Something important had been swirling through her mind all night, keeping her from sleep until the dark early hours. Another yawn forced open her jaw. She stretched out and stared at her wardrobe, where a white dress hung motionlessly like a phantom.

Dress.

White dress.

Wedding dress.

Wedding!

"Why am I still in bed?" Julia cried. "It's my *wedding day!*"

She tossed back the covers and stuffed her feet into her sheepskin slippers, glancing at the alarm clock on the bedside table.

8:13 am.

"No, no, no, *no!*"

Julia should have been up way before the sunrise and the radiators turning on. Why hadn't the alarms blared at 6 am, or 6:01 am, or 6:02 am? She had set three to avoid this very situation.

Skidding on the rug, she snatched her fluffy pink dressing gown off the bedpost and messily dragged it over her pyjamas. She caught her balance, bypassing the dress without daring to give it a second glance.

Leaving Mowgli on the bed, Julia burst into the hallway, and it became instantly apparent that she was the only one who had slept in. Sue, Julia's younger sister and matron of honour, was in the sitting room with Julia's best friend and bridesmaid, Roxy. They had slept over to be there for the early morning wedding preparations.

"What's going on?" Julia shouted, barely able to breathe. "Why didn't you wake me?"

Sue and Roxy jumped up from the couch, staring at her with matching smiles made from equal parts guilt and sympathy.

Julia's eighteen-year-old adopted daughter, Jessie, hurried out of the kitchen, a flour-covered apron over her black silk pyjamas. She opened her hands and held her palms out as though surrendering.

"*Don't* freak out!" Jessie's voice wobbled. "I snuck in and turned your alarms off this morning."

"Why would you do such a thing? It's my *wedding day*! This isn't time for games, Jessie!"

"It's not a game." Jessie bit into her lip as she

9

shuffled on the spot. "There's been an accident."

"What kind of accident?"

"A terrible one," Sue muttered as she crept sheepishly into the hallway. "It was Jessie's idea to turn your alarm off. I wanted to wake you up."

"Wake me up for *what*?"

"The important thing to remember is that it's nobody's fault." Jessie's palms flapped back and forth. "And I'm going to fix it."

"Fix *what*?"

Roxy sighed and followed Sue into the hallway. Julia stared at her with an imploring gaze. If anyone couldn't keep a secret from Julia, it was her oldest school friend.

"I couldn't sleep, so I got up to make some hot chocolate," Roxy began. "I opened the fridge to get the milk, and it seems the fridge broke sometime during the night."

"Okay." Julia nodded, unsure why that mattered. "Is this going somewhere?"

"Your wedding cake," Sue said, the ends of her brows turning down. "It's ruined."

The words hit Julia like a slap across the face. It was awful enough to hear that any cake she had passionately baked was ruined, but her wedding cake?

"Are you sure?" Julia pulled her dressing gown together. "A wedding cake can survive without being refrigerated for a couple of hours. The icing would have protected it."

From their hopeless expressions, Julia knew there was more to the story. Jessie dropped her head and walked into the kitchen, and Roxy and Sue nodded for Julia to follow. Mixing bowls and baking ingredients cluttered every inch of the counters, and it looked like something was in the oven. Jessie stepped back and gestured for Julia to open the fridge.

"I'm really sorry," Jessie said.

Julia's mouth felt like the Sahara as she reached out with a shaky hand and pulled on the door of the dead machine. The scent of warm, sour milk hit her nostrils as soon as the door cracked open.

"What the—" Julia gagged, covering her mouth with the sleeve of her gown.

She let the door swing open to reveal the four-tier white wedding cake with its intricately detailed icing. To the naked eye, it still looked as pristine as it had been when she added the finishing details the night before, but it reeked like it had been left out in the sun for weeks.

"I may have left the cap off the milk," Jessie

11

muttered, *"again."*

Julia gritted her teeth as she looked at the large bottle of soured milk in the inside of the door. How many times had she asked Jessie not to be so lazy when putting the milk back?

"I thought we could air it out?" Roxy offered. "Stick it outside for a bit to get some fresh air, but Jessie said the smell will have stuck to the icing."

"She's right." Julia nodded.

"And I said we couldn't have your wedding guests eating a cake that smells like milk gone off," Sue added. "Especially since you made it yourself. The last thing you want is for your wedding to ruin your reputation as the best baker in Peridale."

"That's why I got to work on a replacement." Jessie glanced at the glowing oven. "I thought I could get it finished before you woke up, but I couldn't find your recipe, and I have no idea what's underneath the icing. I thought about cutting it but—"

"I said that wouldn't be right," Sue jumped in. "Only the bride and groom should cut the cake, spoiled or not."

Julia closed the fridge door, sealing her creation inside its rancid tomb. It felt like she was saying goodbye to a child before it'd had a chance to reach its potential. She loved nothing more than seeing people enjoy her products, but the most important cake of her baking career would never pass anyone's lips.

"*Julia?*" Roxy prompted. "Say something."

Julia took in the mess Jessie had created. She sighed, but she couldn't be angry at her daughter; not today.

"You should have woken me," Julia said, resting her hand on Jessie's shoulder, "but I appreciate you trying to fix it."

"You don't seem upset." Jessie narrowed her eyes as she stepped back. "Why aren't you upset?"

"Poor thing is in shock." Sue rested her hand on Julia's forehead. "She needs some hot, sweet tea. Although it will have to be without the milk, for obvious reasons. Fill the kettle, Roxy!"

"I'm fine." Julia waved her hand to stop Roxy in her tracks. "It's not an ideal situation, but there's no point getting upset about it. Like you said, nobody's to blame for the fridge breaking. I've needed to replace the old thing for years. I bought it for next to nothing from a car boot sale when I first moved in, so if anyone's to blame, it's me for being so cheap."

"I think I'd feel better if you were freaking out," Sue said as she backed out of the kitchen. "You're the calmest I've ever seen a bride on her wedding day."

A small part of Julia wanted to let go and have a meltdown; no one would blame her. Women had slipped into bridezilla mode for much less. It might even make her feel a fraction better to scream and throw the cake through the window, but it wouldn't fix anything. The cake would still be ruined, with her mood joining it. She took a moment to assess the chaos in the kitchen before clapping her hands together.

"I have a plan!" she declared, lightening her tone. "We're wasting valuable time. Jessie, what's in the oven?"

"A vanilla sponge for the base tier."

"Not exactly the fruitcake I had planned, but it's a good start, and it's hard to go wrong with a nice sponge." Julia peered into the oven. "It looks like it's nearly ready. I'll get to work on the other tiers. The sooner they're all baked, the longer they can cool before we try to decorate. If we reduce it to three instead of the original four, it'll save us time." She paused and looked around, her eyes landing on the pantry door. "Jessie, look in there for those tubs of pre-made white icing we bought when you were practising. They should still be in date. They just need rolling out. And I think I have some white icing flowers left over from the cake I made for Shilpa's birthday last week. They should be in a plastic zip-lock bag."

"Got 'em," Jessie called from the cupboard. "There's about two dozen in here. And there's an extra piping bag. I can whip up some royal icing for the detail work."

"Perfect." Julia glanced above the dead fridge at the cat clock with its swinging tail and swishing eyes. "The wedding is at noon, which gives us under four hours to get the cake finished."

"I think I'm going to throw up," Sue groaned.

"We can do this!"

"How long did you spend on the original cake?" Roxy asked.

"Two weeks."

"I'm going to faint." Sue stumbled back and wafted herself. "You shouldn't be worrying about something like this on your wedding day. I bet Barker is still asleep at the B&B without a care in the world. We should be pampering you right now with a glass of bubbly while one of us paints your nails."

"I've never been the biggest fan of champagne," Julia called over her shoulder as she weighed out white flour for the next tier. "Start getting yourselves ready while I do as much as I can in here. Jessie, get the icing rolled out. It needs to be as thin and even as possible. Make it look like it didn't come out of a box."

Jessie cleared a section of the counter and got to work on the icing, while Julia created the batter for the middle chocolate layer. Despite the disarray around her, it was easy for her to slip into her little baking world. The less she thought about the impending ceremony, the less her hands shook as she weighed each ingredient.

Sue and Roxy took it in turns to shower, and it wasn't long before the loud whirring of the hairdryer filled the tiny cottage. It was so loud that Julia almost didn't hear the knocking at the door.

"I'll get it!" she called as she hurried down the hallway, still in her dressing gown.

She dusted her floury hands on her backside and opened the door. The frosty morning air drifted in immediately.

"Flower delivery for a Miss South?" said a young man in a green uniform, his breath turning to steam as he read from an electronic device.

"That's me," Julia said, eagerly peering at the van behind him. "They're my wedding flowers."

The man smiled, but it was clear he had little interest in anything save finishing the delivery. Turning on his heels, he jogged down the path to retrieve three white boxes from the back of his van. He stacked them on the doorstep before holding out the device for Julia to sign. She wiggled her finger on the dotted line, which caused him to hurry away without so much as another word. Too excited to be bothered by his sullen attitude, Julia scooped up the chilled boxes and brought them inside.

"The flowers are here!" she called, kicking the door shut behind her.

She took them into the dining room, and the trio followed. Roxy's fiery red mane was still damp, and Sue's caramel locks were sleekly curled on one side and frizzy on the other.

"I love this part!" Sue squealed. "I remember getting my flowers on my wedding day. They were so perfect."

Julia peeled back the lid, but her flowers were anything but perfect. She dropped the cover onto the table and snatched off the other two.

"This isn't what I ordered," Julia said, her brows dropping as she stared at four bouquets of blood-red roses. "I asked for *cream* roses, just like mum had at her wedding."

Sue and Roxy parted their lips, but neither of them

seemed able to offer anything.

"Call the company!" Jessie demanded. "Who did you use? I'll call them myself!"

"I've already signed for them." Julia pinched the bridge of her nose. "I should have checked first."

She plucked out her bridal bouquet and turned it around in the light. The roses were fresh and fine-looking, but they weren't what she had envisioned for her special day.

"They won't match anything," Julia said as she put the flowers back in their box. "The colour scheme is white and cream."

"Nobody will notice," Roxy offered. "Do people even pay attention to colour schemes?"

"*Yes!*" Sue blurted, causing Roxy to elbow her in the ribs. "I mean, they're adorable. So, you wanted cream roses? It doesn't matter. They're only flowers. It's not what's important today."

"And if they offend you that much, I'm sure Johnny can do some magic on the wedding pictures to turn them cream." Roxy wrapped her arm around Julia's shoulders. "You know he's a computer whiz. Chin up, Julia."

Julia could feel her mind edging closer and closer to the brink of what she could cope with on the morning of her wedding. She wanted nothing more than to cuddle up to Barker, and for him to assure her none of it mattered, but he was the one person she wasn't allowed to see today of all days.

"They're only flowers." Julia echoed. "Beautiful flowers. I have a wedding cake to finish."

Roxy and Sue let out relieved sighs as though they had been holding their breath waiting for Julia's reaction.

"That's the spirit." Sue clapped her hands together. "You've got the wedding day bad luck out of the way early on. Remember how my hair stylist had food poisoning? It's all part of the process. I promise, nothing else can possibly go wrong."

Julia retreated to the kitchen to continue work on the cake. Jessie handed her a cup of peppermint and liquorice tea with a smile. As Julia thought about Sue's promise, soft drops of rain began to fall from the dark sky.

Agatha Frost

2

J ulia had never considered herself a particularly attractive woman. She didn't dislike what she saw in the mirror, but she had never obsessed over her appearance. She was confident enough to leave the house without makeup, and she wasn't too concerned about the pounds that had been contributing to her waistline with each passing birthday. She tried to remember if she had cared in her twenties, but now that she was thirty-nine, her appearance was usually the last thing on her mind.

Julia was happiest when flat shoes cushioned her feet, her curly hair was out of her face, and she was wearing one of her comfortable vintage dresses with an apron over top. If she wanted to wear makeup, it was usually limited to a quick coat of mascara and a berry-toned lip-stain. Occasionally, she would push the boat out to blusher if she looked pale. Fashion trends passed her by without seizing her attention, shopping trips for new clothes and accessories were always at the bottom of her to-do lists, and even when she dressed up for a special occasion, nothing felt better than stripping it away at the end of the night.

Alone in her bedroom, gazing at her reflection, she knew today would not be one of those days. She felt more beautiful than she ever had in all her almost-forty years. The high-heeled shoes weren't exactly comfortable, and she could barely breathe thanks to the dress's built-in girdle, but it didn't matter. Even the heavy bullets of rain pounding against the tiny cottage couldn't shake her elation. If she could bottle the feeling, she would.

The bedroom door creaked open, and Sue snuck back in from her bathroom break. She had spent the past hour transforming Julia's face and hair into the pure, perfect vision of a bride, and she had even helped Julia into her dress, but that didn't stop her from gasping when she saw the finished product.

"Oh, Julia!" Sue clasped her hand against her mouth as tears gathered in the corners of her eyes. "You look just like Mum."

Julia glanced at the picture of their mother on the dresser. Losing her at such a young age had left Julia with few memories to cling to, and even though she hadn't been born when her parents married, their wedding pictures were her most treasured possessions. In their pictures, her parents were so obviously happy and in love.

Julia had only ever wanted a wedding that mirrored her parents' special day. Staring in the mirror, she couldn't deny that she looked more like their mother than she had ever given herself credit for.

"You can't start crying." Julia looked up at the ceiling and blinked rapidly to stem her tears. "You're going to make me cry."

"I know," Sue whined as she scrambled in her handbag for a tissue. "You just look so angelic."

Sue dabbed at her eyes with a tissue before passing it to Julia. As Julia stopped the tears from ruining her perfect makeup, she turned back to the mirror and gazed at her dress. The structured silk and lace bodice hugged her frame in all the right places before flaring out into a subtle A-line, floor-length skirt with a short train. It gave her body a shape that she had always assumed wouldn't be possible without years in the gym.

"Barker is the luckiest man in Peridale." Sue appeared behind Julia and fiddled with the chocolatey curls hanging down from the intricate up-do she had created. "My best work yet."

Julia glanced at the clock, and her stomach performed a small somersault. She would be heading to the church in fifteen minutes to meet her husband-to-be, and even though it had been less than twenty-four hours since they had parted, she was more excited to see him than she had ever been.

"You should change into your dress," Julia said, resting her hand on her stomach. "The cars will be here any minute."

"One last thing." Sue hurried across the room and dug in the bags of makeup and hair products she had brought with her. She pulled out a slender box and placed it on the bed before opening it. "My veil. I thought this could be your something borrowed. It's brought Neil and me six happy years of marriage so far. I know you've bought your own, so you don't have to wear it, but—"

"I'd be honoured." Julia closed her hands around her sister's. "Thank you."

Sue looked as though she was holding back more tears, but, as though for the sake of her mascara, she swallowed them back. She slotted the veil's clip into the back of Julia's hair and fanned out the tulle fabric, which had similar lace detailing as the dress; it matched like they were created for one another by the same hand.

"There's your something borrowed." Sue rested her hands on Julia's shoulders. "What about your old, new, and blue?"

"Mum's engagement ring is old." Julia held up her hand. "And my dress is new."

"And the blue?"

A smile tickled Julia's lips as she reached down to pluck up her dress. She hoisted it up to her upper thigh and gave Sue a sudden flash of her blue garter before letting it drop back down.

"Then you're ready!" Sue chuckled. "I'll leave you and your dress alone while I get into mine."

Sue kissed Julia on the cheek before slipping out of the room. Julia only had another thirty seconds alone with her dress before the door cracked open again and

Roxy's head popped in. She scanned the room, double-taking when she saw Julia.

"*Wow!*" Roxy closed the door behind her, her mobile phone clutched in her fist. "Bloody hell, Julia! If Barker doesn't want to marry you, I don't mind taking his place. You look stunning."

"You don't look so bad yourself." Julia looked Roxy up and down. "I don't think I've seen you in a dress in years."

"Don't get used to it." Roxy brushed down the cream fabric. "Although, I'm grateful you picked pretty bridesmaids' dresses. You could have been a spiteful witch like the rest of them and given us hideous puffy numbers, but I actually feel quite lovely." Roxy looked around the room again before landing on Julia with a shaky smile. "Where's Sue flitted off to?"

"Has something happened?"

"*No!*" Roxy forced a laugh as she made a dismissive gesture with her hands. "Everything is completely *fine!*"

Julia didn't need to say a word. She arched a brow and crossed her arms. Roxy's veneer slipped away instantly; she had never been a good liar.

"There's a *minor* problem with the wedding cars." Roxy patted the phone in her palm. "The riverbank has burst in Riverswick, and the main road is flooded. The

Rolls Royces you booked are stuck there."

Julia inhaled deeply, her fingers drifting up to rub her temples. She could hardly believe something else had gone wrong.

"They can send cars from their other location, but it will take them forty minutes to get here." Roxy glanced at the clock. "And they'll be white Rolls Royces, not the black ones you wanted. They're waiting for me to call back with an answer. I didn't want to bring this to you, but what do you want me to do?"

Julia stared out the window at the grey fog as thick blobs of rain continued to bounce against the glass. She had been specific about wanting black Rolls Royces to take her to the church. It wasn't a long drive, but they were the exact cars Julia's mother had travelled in. She closed her eyes while reminding herself the cars wouldn't matter once they were married.

"We have cars." Julia pushed forward a smile to hide her disappointment. "We'll take my Ford Anglia and Jessie's Mini. It will all be fine."

Roxy looked unsure, but she nodded before leaving the room. Julia tore herself away from the mirror and followed. She picked up the bottom of her dress and carefully made her way into the kitchen, where Jessie was busy piping the finishing details onto the cake. Jessie already wore her cream bridesmaid's dress and her dark brown hair with red highlights was in a similar up-do to Julia's.

"Nearly done," Jessie said without glancing up, wiping sweat from her forehead with the back of her hand. "It's not perfect, but it's the best I can do."

The lines were wobbly and not up to Julia's usual standards. It was a pale imitation of the spoiled cake in the fridge, but it was a serviceable wedding cake. As long as people didn't get too close, it wouldn't look too out of place.

"It's perfect," Julia assured her. "Thank you."

Jessie huffed, looking up for the first time. Her eyes widened when they landed on the dress.

"Check you out, cake lady!" Jessie laughed as she shook her head. "You look so different!"

"Do you like?"

"You look like a bride."

"Thanks, I guess?" Julia laughed. "That's what I was going for."

"But, I mean, a *perfect* bride." Jessie waved the piping bag. "Like from a magazine. You look beautiful. I really mean it."

"You don't look too bad yourself."

Jessie smiled and blushed before returning to her

task. At one time, Jessie wouldn't have been seen out of a black hoody, baggy jeans, and clunky Doc Martens, but she had allowed more colour and fashion into her life since turning eighteen. Still, Julia could tell Jessie didn't feel entirely herself in a dress, no matter how lovely she looked.

A knock sounded at the door, but before Julia could go for it, Sue hurried out of the bathroom, now dressed. She opened it to their father, who was huddled under a large golf umbrella as rain bounced around him.

"Wonderful day for it!" Brian exclaimed, backing into the cottage while letting the umbrella down. "Sorry I'm late. Taxi drivers are striking over their wages all over the Cotswolds. I tried to wait for a gap in the rain to walk, but it doesn't seem like it's going anywhere."

He closed the door and leaned the umbrella against the wall before shaking off a thin raincoat to reveal his three-piece suit. He gazed at Sue and beamed at her beauty, but his eyes drifted straight to Julia when he noticed her at the end of the hall.

"Oh, my baby! Come here. Let me get a better look at you."

Julia shuffled down the hallway, not wanting to trip over the hem of her dress. Her father held his hands out and clutched her shoulders as he looked her up and down. He gulped as though biting back tears. Sniffing hard, he reached into the inside pocket of his suit jacket. He pulled out a red velvet box and cracked it open to reveal a pair of milky pearl earrings.

"They were your mother's," he said with a warm smile. "She wore them on our wedding day."

"Dad. I—"

"To match your ring," he interrupted. "They belong to you now."

Julia removed the tiny diamond studs she had plucked from her messy jewellery box before accepting the velvet box with shaky fingers. She pulled the pearls out of their casing and fitted them into her ears. When she had the backs on, her father hooked his finger under her chin and pointed her face up to the light.

"You look so much like her," he said softly. "She'd be so proud of you."

"I wish she were here," Julia found herself saying. "I miss her most on days like this."

"She's here." He tapped his finger against Julia's chest, right over her heart. "She's always here."

Julia had to clench her jaw to halt the tears threatening to overflow. After placing the red velvet box on the hallway table, she hugged her father tightly.

For that intimate moment, she wasn't a bride on her wedding morning, she was a girl who needed a cuddle from her daddy. No matter how old she grew or how many ups and downs their relationship had endured, no other gesture was able to ease her more.

Roxy, Jessie, and Sue gravitated to the hallway after they had added the finishing touches to their outfits. A pink bottle of sweet perfume made its way around before disappearing into Sue's tiny handbag.

"The cars are cutting it fine," Brian said, checking his watch as he wafted his arm through the fragrance cloud. "It's almost noon."

"They're not coming," Julia explained. "The roads are flooded in Riverswick."

"Those damn roads flood every year!" Brian huffed. "When are the council going to pull their fingers out and fix those riverbanks for good?"

"A question for another day." Julia glanced at the clock on the wall. "We need to set off. We're taking the cars we have. Sue, you can drive Dad and me in my car, and Jessie and Roxy can head down in the Mini."

After grabbing the car keys and all the umbrellas Julia owned, they made their way down the waterlogged garden path. Sue and Roxy scurried behind Julia, lifting her train so it wouldn't drag in the muddy puddles. After Sue unlocked the car doors, Julia climbed onto the backseat, miraculously dry. Roxy stuffed the end of the dress inside before slamming the door shut and hurrying to Jessie's yellow Mini. Sue settled behind the wheel, and their father joined Julia in the back. They sat in silence and looked ahead as the rain drummed against the car's metal roof.

"Ready?" Sue asked as she turned the key in the ignition.

"As I'll ever be." Julia wrapped her hand around her father's. "To the church, driver."

3

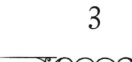

The journey to St. Peter's was a short and silent one. They pulled up outside the church in the heart of the village a couple minutes past noon, and, to Julia's relief, the downpour finally eased to a light drizzle—not that the dark clouds had yet to part.

Sue killed the engine and pulled a compact mirror from her bag. She gave her makeup a once over before passing it to Julia for final checks. Julia looked in the small mirror, but her eyes went straight to the veil instead of her makeup. Her stomach dropped, and for the first time since waking up, it hit her that she was actually about to get married. The string of bad luck had kept her distracted, but now that she was outside the church, she couldn't escape what she was about to do.

"Last chance to change your mind." Sue met Julia's eyes in the rear-view mirror. "Say the word, and I drive us far away from here."

Julia knew her sister was playing with her, but she didn't consider the offer for a second. Nerves aside, she couldn't have been surer that she was doing the right thing.

"Maybe next time." Julia passed the mirror back before inhaling deeply. "I'm ready to become Mrs South-Brown."

Under a canopy of giant umbrellas, they hastily made their way to the entrance of the church, where the front doors already stood open for them. Once safe and dry in the vestibule, the bridesmaids fussed around Julia, adjusting her dress and hair. When they were satisfied that she was perfect, Roxy slipped into the church to announce their arrival. The chatter from the guests died down instantly.

"*Wait!*" a familiar voice cried.

Julia spun around as her eighty-four-year-old gran, Dot, hurried into the church under the protection of an umbrella—not that she needed it, thanks to her bright yellow hat, twice the width of her slender frame.

"I lost track of time!" Dot panted as she caught her breath and collapsed the umbrella. "Oh, look at you, Julia! Perfection!"

"Thanks, Gran," Julia replied with a smile as Dot kissed her on both cheeks. "Although, maybe you should go and join the choir for your big debut before they start without you."

"Righty-oh!" Dot wagged her finger before scurrying to the doors that led to the nave. "Wish me luck!"

Seconds later, another elderly member of the Peridale Harmonics Choir, Percy Cropper, hurried into the church with a tea towel over his bald head. The comical, rotund man dabbed at his face as he smiled his apologies for his lateness before tossing the towel onto the table containing the church activities flyers.

"Very lovely," he said quickly to Julia before following Dot into the church.

Sue glanced over her shoulder at Julia and the sisters shared a quick smile. They'd had their suspicions that an unlikely romance had been blossoming between their gran and Percy since she had joined the choir. The tea towel from Dot's kitchen all but confirmed it.

Seconds later, the deep and lively notes of the organ filled the air. The doors into the church opened from within, revealing the rows of guests waiting patiently for a glimpse of the bride. They rose to their feet as the choir began to sing. Taking their signal, Sue, Roxy, and Jessie set off, walking down the aisle in a neat line.

"Ready?" Brian whispered after kissing her temple.

Julia nodded. He pulled the veil over her face and held out his arm. She gratefully looped hers through his; her knees were suddenly unable to fully support her weight in the heavy dress. Gulping down her fear, she clung tight to her father. Her feet moved forward, not that she had any control over them. She was sure it was the closest to an out-of-body experience she would ever experience.

The guests all turned to gaze at Julia, their faces all wearing the same doe-eyed expression. Cameras flashed, capturing her from every angle. Despite the weather, the turnout appeared strong.

Her old school friends, newspaper editor, Johnny Watson, and wedding planner, Leah Burns, were the first faces she saw. They held hands, showing how in love they had grown since they had started dating at the end of the summer. Their familiar smiles eased her nerves a little.

Her eyes danced over the faces of the Peridale residents she had invited. They all smiled at her, some of them dabbing their watery eyes. She hoped she was smiling back behind the veil because she couldn't seem to control any part of her body as she drifted closer to the front of the church. Sue's husband, Neil, held their twin baby girls, Pearl and Dottie, who were being remarkably quiet in their pretty pink dresses. Julia's father's wife, Katie, was in the front row of Julia's side of the church, with Julia's baby brother, Vinnie, wriggling in her arms. He looked adorable in his tiny tuxedo, grinning under his mop of dark curls.

Barker's side was filled with people from his book publishing company and former colleagues from the police station. The only family member who had returned the RSVP—his eldest brother, Casper—stood next to Barker as his best man. Casper's wife, Heather, proudly grinned from the front row.

Julia looked at the choir, who were harmonising with the organ, their 'oohs' and 'ahhs' floating around the grand building. Julia's gran and Jessie's brother,

Alfie, were stood in the back row, sharing the same delighted smile as they watched her walk.

Julia's eyes finally landed on Barker's back. He was looking straight ahead at the altar, his hands clasped behind him. Casper noticed Julia and patted Barker on the shoulder with his free hand; his other clutched the cane he needed to support his prosthetic leg.

Barker spun around, a broad smile captivating her attention. She returned it, and the world melted away. It didn't matter that the cake wasn't perfect, or that the cars hadn't arrived, or that the flowers were the wrong colour, or that it was raining; this was why she was here. This man. This moment.

When Julia reached the end of the aisle, her father let go and stepped to the side to join Katie. She felt like she was floating in a dream state behind her hazy veil as Barker's gaze pulled her in to join him. Once she was in position, he lifted her veil, freeing her to take him in unobstructed.

"You look amazing," he whispered, his smile beaming from ear-to-ear. "Nervous?"

"Not anymore," she said, looking deep into his eyes.

They held hands and turned to Father David, who smiled down at them from a raised platform. Thunder rumbled outside. As Julia had requested, the choir began to sing 'All Things Bright and Beautiful', mirroring the song the very same choir had sung for her mother and father on their special day over forty years ago.

The choirmaster, Gloria Gray, stepped forward to take the lead vocals of the hymn. Somewhere in her late sixties, Gloria was a tall and wide woman with a commanding presence. Short grey curls sprouted from her head in all directions, and even though her round face was soft and pale, her gaze carried the authority of a woman in charge. She had been Julia's music teacher at St. Peter's Primary School, and she had always caused an irrational fear deep within Julia. Even as a child, Julia hadn't sensed any warmth within the woman.

Despite this, Julia was glad to have Gloria singing at her wedding. She was the longest-serving member of the choir; more than once, she had told Julia she had been part of the choir that had sung at Julia's parents' wedding all those years ago.

Julia glanced up at the cavernous ceiling. Was her mother up there looking down on them? Thunder signalled again. She wasn't sure she believed in heaven, but she was happy to believe in it today.

Hand in hand, Julia and Barker watched the choir sing. Dot and Alfie provided backing vocals, but Gloria seemed to be the only member actually singing. It felt less like a choral performance and more like a singer with her back-up. Her vocals bellowed into every corner of the church without the aid of a microphone.

"You're not wearing your wedding suit," Julia whispered to Barker when she noticed that he was wearing a dark blue, pinstriped business jacket.

"It's a long story," he whispered back. "I'll explain later. I've had a string of bad luck this morning."

"I'm glad it wasn't just me then."

"You too?" He squeezed her hand. "The universe can do whatever it wants. Nothing is going to stop us marrying today."

The choir reached the climax of the song, but to Julia's surprise, Gloria fluffed the final high note. She choked and began to cough, much to the horror of the rest of the choir. Amy Clark abruptly stopped playing the organ, sending the church into silence. Gloria looked around, her eyes wide. She appeared as though she was about to apologise, but a short, impish woman with wiry grey hair pulled her back. Gloria shrugged the other woman off and sat with a huff.

The awkward silence that followed was interrupted

when Gloria struggled back more coughing. She reached under the bench for a water bottle, which she took a deep swig from. Barker glanced at Julia, but all she could offer was a shrug.

"Wasn't that lovely?" Father David offered an unsure smile as he stepped forward. "Thank you to the Peridale Harmonics Choir for another divine performance."

He cleared his throat and tugged at his dog collar before opening his order of service. His lips parted, but before he could start, Gloria's coughing cut him off.

"*Dearly beloved,*" Father David bellowed over the noise, "we are gathered here today in the sight of God to witness the union of Barker Fergus Brown and Julia Maria South in holy—"

Gloria spluttered as she drank more water, before breaking into an even louder coughing fit. All eyes turned to her, including Father David's. Other members of the choir looked away, obviously embarrassed. Dot rolled her eyes, and it seemed only the impish lady Julia didn't know cared about comforting Gloria.

"*—in holy matrimony,*" Father David continued, "which is an honourable estate, that is not to be entered into unadvisedly or—"

Gloria's coughing interrupted him once again. Father David sighed and snapped the order of service shut before turning to the choir.

"Maybe you should excuse yourself, Gloria?" he whispered. "Get some fresh air?"

Gloria nodded and stood up, but more coughing made her stumble back and fall onto Dot and Alfie. They let out identical yelps as the weight of the heavy woman crashed down on them. A gasp echoed around the church, followed by disapproving chatter.

"She doesn't look good," Julia whispered to Barker as Gloria regained her balance. "Her face is turning purple."

Gloria walked along the row, coughing the whole way. She staggered down a step and looked out at the congregation with pleading eyes. Sweat rolled down her flushed face. Julia clutched Barker's hand as other members of the choir exited to surround her. A handful of guests stood up, but nobody seemed to know what to do. A collective cry boomed through the room when Gloria dropped to her knees.

"Somebody *help* her!" the impish woman cried desperately. "She can't *breathe!*"

Father David hurried over and rested his hand on Gloria's back before looking up helplessly and crying,

"Is there a doctor in attendance?"

There was a moment of desperate silence as the guests looked amongst themselves, waiting for a medical professional to come forward; none did.

"I'm a nurse," Sue called as she passed her flowers to Roxy. "Let me take a look."

But Sue didn't reach Gloria in time to do anything. Gloria slouched forward and clutched Father David's white robes, coughing one last time before dropping to the ground on her front with a silencing thud. Everyone gulped, including Julia and Barker, when they saw the tiny red splatters of blood on the vicar's robes.

Sue dropped down and dug two fingers into Gloria's fleshy neck as Father David and the rest of the choir backed away. Sue stared at Julia, her expression grave.

"I think she's dead."

Agatha Frost

4

The sun seemed to set extra early that night. Julia and Barker stood in their kitchen as the light disappeared around them. Still in their wedding outfits, they had been staring mutely at the wedding cake leaning against the counter for the past hour. Julia was too in shock to attempt to remove the dress on her own.

The house phone rang on the kitchen wall for the thirteenth time since they had returned to the cottage.

They had ignored it each time, but Julia couldn't stand to listen to it ring anymore. She left Barker's side and snatched the phone line out of the wall before immediately retreating to his side. He wrapped his arm around her shoulders and pulled her in.

"The cake is missing a tier," Barker finally said, breaking the silence that had been bubbling since they had left the police station.

"The fridge broke and ruined the original one," she explained, her voice numb. "We made this one this morning. Quickly."

Julia reached out and dug her fingers into the middle tier. She pulled out a fistful of the cake and took a large bite. It was the first thing she had eaten all day.

"Double chocolate fudge cake," Julia explained after swallowing her first mouthful. "You might as well help yourself. No point wasting good cake."

Barker looked unsure, but she gave him an encouraging nod. He broke off a chunk of the cake, and they resumed their position leaning against the counter and staring into space while they ate.

"It's delicious," Barker said between bites.

"I wanted to surprise you with your favourite." Julia glanced at the clock. "Our reception would have been starting in ten minutes. We'd have been cutting the cake as husband and wife in a couple of hours."

She sighed and finished her cake. When she was done, she licked her fingers instead of washing them; she didn't have the energy for manners.

"That poor woman," Barker said quietly. "I can't believe she just keeled over and died like that."

Julia couldn't shake the image of Gloria lying dead on the church floor. She had remained there for an hour thanks to flooding rerouting the ambulance. Sue had spent a good chunk of that hour diligently trying to revive her with CPR. Father David had finally pulled Sue away, telling her it was in God's hands now.

"Do you believe in omens?" she asked.

"I don't know."

"I think I do after today." Julia wiped the crumbs from her face with the back of her hand. "Someone or something out there didn't want us to get married. They threw everything in our way to stop us. The fridge broke and ruined the wedding cake, my flowers weren't the ones I ordered, the wedding cars were stuck in a flood."

"And my suit." Barker looked down at his pinstriped jacket. "I burned a hole in mine with the iron. Evelyn knocked on every door in the B&B until she found a guest who owned a suit. This was all they had."

"Maybe we should have listened." Julia rubbed between her eyes. "The signs were there."

"It was just bad luck."

"Bad luck is missing a bus. Today was something biblical. I'm surprised my dress didn't burst into flames to really hammer the message home."

Barker's forehead creased as he offered Julia a sympathetic smile. She felt like she was on the verge of tears, but she didn't have the energy to produce any, so she laughed. She laughed until Barker started laughing. They held each other and laughed away their pain in the middle of the kitchen, only breaking away when a key rattled in the front door.

"*Mum?*" Jessie's voice bellowed down the hallway. "*Barker?*"

Soaked from the rain, Jessie ran into the kitchen. She immediately slapped the light switch, blinding Julia and Barker in the process.

"I've been waiting at the station for you!" Jessie whacked her clutch bag down on the counter. "I was worried sick! I thought you'd run away."

"That doesn't sound like such a bad idea right now." Julia pulled off her veil and began to pluck the masses of pins Sue had used out of her hair. "We didn't mean to worry you. We needed some alone time to come to terms with not becoming husband and wife."

"I'm so sorry," Jessie offered as she scratched the back of her neck. "I have no idea what to say. Why don't I help you get out of that dress?"

Julia nodded. She looked down at her once perfect dress. The hem was muddy and frayed from the rain, and chocolate crumbs spattered the bodice. It reminded her of the blood splatters on Father David's white robes. She wanted her earlier euphoria to return, but she doubted this—or any other—dress would arouse such a feeling in her again.

In the bathroom, Jessie unlaced the corset and helped Julia wriggle out of the garment. Leaving Julia in her underwear, Jessie whisked the dress away and returned with a set of fluffy pink pyjamas. Without asking if she wanted one, Jessie pulled the shower curtain across the bathtub and turned on the hot water. She kissed Julia on the cheek before slipping out.

Julia stared at herself in the mirror. Her perfect makeup had run and faded, and her intricate hair hung awkwardly around her face. After stripping off her underwear, she climbed into the shower. She stood directly under the water and let its sizzling heat wash away the day.

Instead of this being the happiest day of her life, she felt only numb.

Time ground to a halt and each second felt like an hour passing. She stood under the water, hugging her body and shivering despite the heat for what felt like a lifetime. She remained unmoving until the hot water ran cold, and, even then, she didn't immediately move. It wasn't until a voice in the back of her mind said, "what are you doing, Julia?" that she cut off the water and climbed out.

As she dried off, voices drifted under the door. At first, she assumed Jessie and Barker were chatting, but she quickly realised the noise was coming from more than two sources. With her wet hair pulled back into a ponytail, she climbed into her pyjamas and finally left the bathroom. She was surprised to see her entire family filling the sitting room.

"Here she is!" Dot jumped up, a glass of champagne in her hand, still wearing her outfit and hat from earlier. "I was about to come and check that you hadn't drowned in there."

"What's all this?" Julia asked, hugging her body, feeling exposed in front of her full house.

"It seemed a shame to waste all the food from the reception," Sue said, holding up a paper plate. "It was all made, so we decided to bring it up here to keep you company."

"Or take your mind off things," her father jumped in.

"You shouldn't be alone at a time like this," Katie added, bouncing Vinnie up and down on her knee. "You need your family here with you."

"And don't worry about this being in bad taste," Dot mumbled through a mouthful of a sandwich. "I know we shouldn't speak ill of the dead, but Gloria was a piece of work. Very few tears will be shed over her tonight."

"*Gran!*" Sue cried. "Time and place."

"I'm only *saying!*" Dot held up her hands. "It's the truth! I've only been part of the choir for a month, and even I could see that she had made enemies of everyone. I wasn't far off becoming one of them! Silly woman said I couldn't keep pitch! Can you believe that? *Me?* I won *Miss Singing Peridale 1953*, I'll have you know! My vocals moved the judges to tears. I could have been a recording artist. They said I had a voice for the radio!"

"Are you sure they didn't say 'face for radio', mother?" Brian lifted his champagne flute and winked before turning to Julia. "If you want us to go, we'll get out of your hair."

Julia smiled her appreciation, even though all she really wanted to do was climb into bed and pretend the whole sorry day had been nothing more than a bad dream. Still, she was happy to see them. It wasn't like she hadn't planned to spend the day with them already.

"Stay," Julia assured them, pushing forward a smile. "Enjoy the food."

"Grab yourself something." Dot wafted her hand towards the dining room. "It's a fabulous spread! These tuna vol-au-vents are to *die* for!"

Leaving Dot to think about her poor choice of words, Julia walked into the dining room, where Barker was deep in conversation with his brother, Casper.

"You *must* have them!" Barker exclaimed, putting a hand to his forehead. "This is the *last* thing we need!"

Casper's wife, Heather, a short, round woman with neat, roller-set grey curls, ushered Julia into the corner of the room.

"You poor thing." Heather pulled Julia down into a tight hug. "My heart breaks for you. You're so strong. How are you holding yourself together?"

"Barely." Julia pulled away with a smile, her focus going straight back to the arguing men. "What's happened?"

"The rings seem to have been misplaced."

"*Misplaced?*" Barker roared. "Casper *lost* them! You have three jobs as a best man! Organise a stag party, give a speech that isn't too embarrassing, and don't lose the rings! Since I didn't want a stag and you got out of the speech, *where* are the rings?"

"Don't take *that* tone with me!" Casper roared back, his entire weight on his cane. "I *told* you! They were in my pocket, and now they're gone. I haven't reached for them since I put them there! In case you hadn't noticed, there have been more important things going on!"

There was an almost thirty-year age gap between Barker and Casper. Their mother had Casper in her late teens, while she'd been in her forties when Barker was born. She'd have been Dot's age if she was still alive, but she had died before reaching her eighties. Despite the age gap, Casper was the only one of Barker's three brothers he was still close to. Casper and Heather had been a couple before Barker was born, and had acted as secondary parents to him throughout his life; something Barker had always appreciated, given he didn't know who his father was.

"Don't get yourself worked up, dear." Heather reached out a hand. "It's been a long day."

Julia looked down at the engagement ring that hugged her finger. It upset her that the wedding band that should have been above it was now missing, but it felt like the tip of the wedding-related-problems iceberg.

"I'm sure they'll show up," Julia offered, sandwiching herself between the two men. "Casper, did you have the jacket on all day?"

"*Yes!*" he cried. "Well, I took it off in the church when we were waiting for the ambulance to turn up, but then I put it right back on when we left."

"And did you check to see if the rings were still there?" she asked.

"Well, no." Casper frowned. "I was too busy thinking about the dead woman on the floor."

"Then they probably slipped out." Julia smiled at him, hoping to calm him down. "And, if that's the case, they'll make their way back to us."

"It still *technically* means he lost them," Barker muttered under his breath.

"Not helping, Barker," Heather called from the corner. "Why don't we all just relax and eat some of this delicious-looking food? It's been a long day for all of us. What will we gain from turning on each other? We should be grateful to be alive right now. Now, shake hands, and we'll revisit the topic when the dust has settled."

Casper huffed but held his hand out. Barker pretended not to notice, prompting Julia to slap him on the arm with the back of her hand. He puffed out his chest and pouted, but he shook his brother's hand, if not a little reluctantly.

"I'm sorry," Barker murmured. "I'm a little tired."

"Some things never change." Casper patted Barker on the cheek. "You always did come over cranky when you were tired, but considering everything else you've been through today, I won't hold it against you."

Heather gathered two plates of food before departing the room with Casper in tow. When they were alone, Julia and Barker hugged again. His exhaustion radiated against her. It gave her an odd comfort; he was the only person who was going through the same thing she was.

"DI Christie called when you were in the shower," Barker said as he rested his head on hers. "He's treating Gloria's death as suspicious."

"Murder?"

"He seems to think so." Barker pulled away, his jaw clenching. "People don't really just drop dead like that, do they?"

"Sometimes." Julia sighed. "But I'd be lying if I thought that's what happened." She paused and cast an eye over the food, but eating was the last thing on her mind. "It happened so quickly. One second she was fine, and then she was choking on her own breath."

Sue crept into the room with an empty plate. She smiled sympathetically at them as she piled up more food.

"This doesn't mean you aren't getting married." Sue broke the silence as she grabbed a handful of cocktail sausages. "You could go to the register office tomorrow and do it. You wouldn't even have to tell anyone."

Julia had been so focussed on the ruined wedding that she hadn't given a second attempt at a wedding a moment of her time. She considered it, but a niggling feeling in the back of her mind confirmed her feelings towards the idea.

"It wouldn't feel right," Julia said, clutching Barker's hand. "At least, not until we know for sure what happened to Gloria."

"I agree." Barker squeezed her hand. "I want you to be my wife more than anything, but not like this. We need to start our marriage on the right foot."

Sue rested her hand on her heart as she munched

through a sausage and said, "You two are the cutest that ever were. Do I still get to be a bridesmaid at the next one?"

"I'll think about it."

Sue winked and left the room with her food. They weren't alone for more than a couple of seconds before Dot shuffled in, with someone new accompanying her. Julia examined the tiny woman glued to Dot's side. She was the choir member Julia had thought of as being impish, and the only one who had seemed concerned by Gloria's coughing. She had sobbed by Gloria's side until the ambulance arrived.

She appeared to be in her seventies and was as short as a child. Her wiry hair hung limply around her face, crying out for a good cut. She was swaddled in a large coat that drowned her petite frame, and an equally oversized, colourful scarf was wrapped around her neck right up to her chin. An overwhelming number of badges and pins cluttered the front of her coat, their enamel coatings catching the light.

"Julia, this is Flora," Dot explained. "Flora Hill. She's a member of the choir."

"Been a member for thirty years," Flora added as she dabbed at her tears with a lace handkerchief that contrasted against her black, fingerless gloves. "I hope you don't mind me turning up like this."

"Not at all." Julia smiled at the woman, but Flora didn't look up. Julia turned to Dot, who merely shrugged before leaving the room. "Barker, why don't you make Mrs Hill a cup of tea?"

"*Miss* Hill," she corrected after blowing her nose. "A cup of tea would be so kind. Plenty of milk and five sugars."

"*Five?*" Barker echoed. Julia gave him a stern look and jerked her head to the door. "Okay, I'm going!"

Julia pulled two chairs from underneath the food-covered table and motioned for Flora to sit. Flora hesitated for a moment, her eyes darting around the room, and then at all the food.

"Do you mind?" Flora asked as she plucked out a sandwich. "I haven't eaten today."

"Help yourself."

"Thank you." Flora devoured the sandwich in a couple of mouthfuls before helping herself to a second. It reminded Julia of how Mowgli devoured turkey slices on Christmas Day. "I'm desperately sorry about what happened today. I never married. Never even got close. I can't imagine how you're feeling right now. You must be devastated."

"That's one word for it."

Flora reached for another sandwich, and then another. She gobbled each down as fast as the last. Barker snuck in and placed the sugary tea next to her, which she gulped back without pausing for breath. Barker looked at Julia for an explanation, but all she could do was lift her shoulders in a half-shrug.

"What must you think of me!" Flora wafted her hanky around before dabbing at her eyes one final time. She jammed the handkerchief deep into her coat pocket. "I'm not myself right now. I'm in shock. Yes, that's what it is. Shock. It must be."

"It's completely normal," Julia said, resting her hand on Flora's knee, which caused her to jerk back. Julia pulled her hand away, but Flora remained tense. "Were you close to Gloria?"

"She is my friend," Flora said, her eyes widening as she stared at the patterns on the carpet. "*Was* my friend. My *only* friend. My *best* friend."

"I'm sorry for your loss."

"How do I go on?" Flora's eyes snapped onto Julia's. "I can't imagine life without her. I have *no one*. Gloria was my only companion in life. Well, there was William, but he died last month."

"William?"

"My cat." Flora's tears flowed again. "William

Shakespaw. He was a stray. I took him in as a kitten. Poor little ginger thing sat on my doorstep for days on end. I kept throwing him scraps. He kept coming back, and he never left. Vets said it was an achievement to get to eighteen, but no amount of time is enough."

Julia's lips parted but she didn't know what to say to comfort the woman. She felt for Flora. Julia had taken Mowgli in as a stray and loved him like a child. Julia picked up another tray of sandwiches and offered them to the weeping woman. Flora plucked out two and gobbled them down in a flash.

"Thank you," Flora said after letting out a small burp. "You're too kind. You shouldn't have to listen to me prattle on, but I had to see you. People said you were the only woman in Peridale capable of finding out the truth."

"Oh, I don't know about—"

"You've solved so many mysteries." Flora dove forward and grabbed both of Julia's hands in her scratchy gloves. "You *must* have a lead!"

"I haven't really given it much thought yet."

"Right." Flora pulled her hands away and nodded. "Of course. I'm sorry. I'm being presumptuous. Gloria always said that was my downfall. I'm too quick to lean on people. She said it was because my parents abandoned me as a child." Flora retrieved her handkerchief and dabbed at her eyes. "I should go. I shouldn't have intruded."

Flora stood up and headed for the door. A small part of Julia wanted to let the woman leave, but a bigger part knew she couldn't.

"Flora, wait." Julia ushered the tiny woman back to her seat. "You're not intruding. Tell me about Gloria. You must be the person who knew her the best."

"I was." Flora nodded before blowing her nose again. "Nobody knew the *real* Gloria, except for me. She put up a front to the world. She was meticulous and exact, and that rubbed people the wrong way. People feel threatened when a woman knows what she wants. They called her bossy, but if she were a man, nobody would have batted an eyelid. They would have called her strong. Instead, they called her every name under the sun, but never to her face. Oh, *never* to her face! Always whispering behind her back. She knew, but she didn't care. Great leaders don't. She directed that choir for decades, and yet not a single one was ever grateful. It would have fallen to pieces dozens of times if she hadn't been there. She was the glue that held them together. I bet they're all partying as we speak, happy their leader is dead."

"Do you think any of them had any reason to want Gloria dead?"

"*Absolutely!*" Flora tucked her hanky away, suddenly sitting up straight. "All of them had their run-ins with Gloria at least once, but none more than that *dreadful* woman, Rita Bishop!" She paused for breath, her lips curling. "Rita joined the choir five years ago, but she's been gunning for Gloria's position since the second she walked in. She thinks because she has a degree she's qualified to lead. She's a stuck-up snob if ever I've met one! She would argue that the sky was green until the cows came home! Gloria couldn't make a single decision without Rita sticking her nose in. I often wondered why Rita stuck around when she obviously wasn't wanted, but now I know. She's been waiting for this day so she could muscle her way in. She was already talking about finding a new leader as they were carrying poor Gloria out of the church!" Flora paused for breath and grabbed Julia's hands again. "You *have* to help me! *Promise* you'll help."

Julia didn't feel comfortable promising such a thing to a woman so clearly distressed, but how could she refuse? If Gloria had dropped dead in the middle of anyone else's wedding, Julia might have been able to step back and let the police figure it out, but it hadn't been anyone else's wedding; it had been hers.

"I can't promise," Julia said, her voice wobbling, "but I will try."

"You *will*?" Flora cried. "Oh, *thank you*! Thank you so much, Julia! I *know* you can do this. I have faith in you. I really will get out of your hair now. You've lifted my spirits." Flora looked back at the table. "Do you mind if I take a sandwich for the road?"

"Let me grab you a box," Julia replied with a smile. "We'll never eat all this between us."

Julia retrieved one of her cardboard cake boxes from the kitchen and watched Flora fill it to the brim with handfuls of everything she could reach.

"I *know* you can do this," Flora said as she scurried into the night with half the buffet in her hands. "Thank you, Julia!"

Julia closed the front door and leaned against it, listening to her family chatter in the sitting room. She closed her eyes, waiting to wake up any moment. When she opened them, she was still firmly in her hallway.

"What did she want?" Dot asked when Julia walked into the sitting room. "She's always been a freaky little woman."

"She wants me to look into Gloria's death."

"Of course, she does!" Dot waved her hands

dramatically. "Flora has always been stuck to Gloria's side! She followed her around like a little lapdog."

"And are you going to do it?" Sue asked, arching a brow. "Don't you think you've got enough on your plate?"

"I said I would." Julia shrugged and ran her fingers through her damp ponytail. "The café is closed for the next week. I wanted us to enjoy our first week of being married at home. If I open, I'm going to have to deal with all the pity looks and questions, so I might as well put my week off to good use."

"And those answers could come tomorrow," Sue said, exhaling. "Let the police do their jobs."

"And if they do, nothing has been lost," Julia replied. "But until then, it won't hurt to gather some information. I don't think I'll be able to settle until we have some answers."

"Julia's right." Barker stood beside her, wrapping his arm around her waist. "This happened at *our* wedding. We have a responsibility to at least try to figure out what happened."

"Then count me in!" Dot slapped her knee and stood up. "What do you say, Alfie? We can snoop around the choir. I'd bet my pension one of them did it!"

"I suppose so," Alfie said, wiping his mouth after taking a bite of a sausage roll. "I'm up for helping."

"Then it's settled." Barker pulled Julia in closer. "Now, we appreciate you all showing your support, but I think my almost-wife and I need some space."

"Say no more." Brian stood up and lifted Vinnie off Katie's knee. "It's this one's bedtime anyway. We'll get out of your hair. Call us if you need anything."

Julia valued Barker for being the one to prompt them to leave. She would never have been able to say anything, and even though she relished spending time with her family, tonight was not the night to sit around until the early hours waiting for Dot to finish the last drops of champagne.

They left one by one, each taking a tray of food at Julia's request. Jessie lingered by the door, still in her bridesmaid's dress.

"I can spend the night at Billy's." She hooked her thumb over her shoulder to the door. "You probably want to be alone."

"Don't be silly." Julia pulled her into the sitting room. "You're not going anywhere tonight. I need your snarky quips to cheer me up."

Without being prompted, Barker built a roaring fire and put on one of Julia's favourite DVDs, *Breakfast at Tiffany's.* The three of them cuddled up under a giant fluffy blanket, Mowgli sprawled in front of the fire, and for the rest of the evening, Julia left her world and lost herself in Audrey Hepburn and George Peppard's on-screen chemistry.

5

J ulia spent the entirety of the next day in her pyjamas. She barely moved from the couch, choosing instead to watch Sunday television from under the warm safety of a blanket. She watched a marathon of people going to other people's homes for dinner and rating them, and a slew of property buying and selling programs.

Jessie brought her regular cups of peppermint and liquorice tea, and Barker intercepted every knock at the door. They had fish and chips delivered for dinner, and by the end of the night, they were all on the couch again, this time watching Barker's favourite film, *Die Hard*.

The telephone remained unplugged, and all mobile phones were switched off. The events of the previous day were never mentioned, and even though Julia couldn't ignore the heavy feeling in her chest, it was easier than she had expected to pretend nothing had happened. When she finally crawled into her warm bed at half past ten, after a bubble bath, she wondered why she hadn't spent more days of her life so cut-off and relaxed.

On Monday morning, which was also Bonfire Night, Julia's eyes sprung open at eight, just like they would have if she were opening the café. She got as far as making herself toast before she remembered what had happened, and that was only because she opened the broken fridge to grab the butter.

She stared at her first wedding cake. The cake that never was for the wedding that didn't happen. It taunted her, urging her to spend another day on the couch. It had been years since she had watched weekday morning television. Were the same faces still lingering around, or had they been replaced with fresher, younger ones?

"If I do," she said to herself as she closed the fridge, "I might never move again."

Instead, she quietly dressed and left the cottage, leaving Barker and Jessie asleep. The chilly morning air filled her lungs, refreshing her after a full day of stuffy radiator heat. Though she had her car keys in hand, she decided to walk and stretch her legs, instead. When she reached the centre of the village, her heart was pumping, and her mind was revitalised.

With a renewed sense of self, Julia hurried down the alley between her beloved café and the post office. She rarely used the back entrance, but just this once, she didn't want people to know she was there.

After turning on the kitchen lights—keeping the front ones switched off—she got to work. She had no idea what she wanted to bake, but a need deep within compelled her to create something. If not to level her mind, then to stop the rushed wedding cake being the last thing she had made.

Her fingers worked automatically, with her mind taking a backseat. Baking was the best free therapy she had access to, and, an hour later, she had twenty neat gingerbread biscuits decorated like fireworks to show for her efforts. She hadn't planned on celebrating

Bonfire Night, so the colourful biscuits brought a smile to her face.

With no intention of opening the café, Julia boxed her work, ready to walk back home to the safety of her cottage. That changed when she received a text message from Dot, via Alfie's phone, that an emergency Peridale Harmonics Choir meeting was happening at the church in 'five minutes!!!!!!!!!'.

Julia stared at the message, unsure of what to do. Could she step foot back into the church where her wedding had been ruined by a woman's death? Her curiosity tingled, but so did the call home. She glanced at the box in her hand; she would enjoy her creation more if she could share it with a group of people.

Leaving the café behind, she walked across the village green to St. Peter's Church. Aside from the police car stationed outside, there were no other signs of what had happened. The choir, including Alfie and Dot, were already milling around in the vestibule when Julia walked in. Dot immediately spotted her and dragged her into a quiet corner.

"Rita called the meeting at the crack of dawn!" Dot whispered, looking around at the other members. "She telephoned us all to let us know the police had finally released the church and that she wanted to meet to discuss our future. I'd ask who died and put her in charge, but we all know the answer to that one. She's going to steamroll everyone and promote herself to leader."

"Can she do that?"

"Who's going to stop her?" Dot cast an eye at the other members. Her eyes lingered on Flora, who was standing on tiptoes to read the signs on the noticeboard. "They're a bunch of wet lemons. I'd put *myself* forward, but I've only been here a month. I only really joined to sing at your wedding. If I weren't undercover trying to suss out which of these old codgers bumped Gloria off, I'd have thrown in my sheet music already!"

"You're probably the oldest here, Gran."

"In age, yes." Dot pushed up her tight grey curls. "But in spirit? The old ticker still has many hours left on the clock. Don't count me out just yet, dear. I'm going to crack this case before you do! You'll see."

"I don't doubt it." Julia chuckled, casting her eye over the members. She recognised Alfie and Flora, as well as Shilpa Patil from the post office and Evelyn Wood from the B&B. Amy Clark, the regular church organist, was also a member, along with Dot's unexpected love interest, Percy Cropper.

There was also a young, beautiful woman with sandy hair, eyes like a doe's, and full lips. Julia would have put the English rose beauty in her late twenties. She stood so close to Alfie that their arms were touching.

"Who's she?" Julia asked, nodding at the girl. "I don't recognise her."

"That's Skye," Dot said after spinning around to look. "Don't know her surname, but I think Alfie has a thing for her. Poor fella gets tongue-tied whenever she enters a room."

"Did she sing at the wedding?"

Dot's nose scrunched up as she thought about it. Julia cast her mind back to the fateful day, but she didn't remember noticing the young woman, and she was sure she would have remembered such a beauty if she had been there.

"I rushed in late, so I can't be sure," Dot said, her finger tapping on her chin, "but now that you mention it, I don't remember seeing her."

"What's she like?"

"She may be young, but she's feisty. Nobody stood up to Gloria like she did! They had a huge argument during our last rehearsal."

"What did they argue about?"

"Oh, the usual humdrum." Dot waved her hand. "Skye wanted a solo, Gloria wouldn't give her one. Skye wanted to take it to a vote, but Gloria's style was hardly diplomatic. Dictator comes to mind, actually. Kim Jong Un would have struggled getting a word in with Gloria Gray!"

"Who do you think would have won the vote?"

"Skye, for sure!" Dot announced. "No doubt about it! Her voice is something else. Gloria might have had the experience, but Skye has the raw talent. I see a lot of myself in her, as it happens." Dot wriggled her brooch with a soft smile. "She could go professional. Did I mention that I won—"

"*Miss Singing Peridale 1953?*" Julia jumped in. "Only every day since you joined the choir."

"It's a shame they don't hold the competition anymore." Dot sighed wistfully, her eyes drifting off. "I fought off my competition like a true champion."

"How many people were you up against?"

"Oh, I can't remember that, dear." Dot pursed her lips and waved her hand. "I've lived many lives since then."

"What did you sing?"

"*How Much Is That Doggie in the Window?*" Dot replied instantly. "I was note-perfect!"

"Selective memory, I see," Julia teased.

At that moment, the church doors burst open, and a sunglasses-adorned, redheaded woman stormed in. She wore a black turtleneck that snaked up to her jawline, with a pearl necklace over the fabric. A floor-length, fur-lined, red-tartan cardigan billowed behind her, so long it would have dragged across the floor if not for the black heels on her feet. If Julia had to guess, she would have put the woman between forty-five and fifty. Julia recognised her from the wedding, but she hadn't paid her much attention.

"*This way*, Harmonics!" the woman demanded as she walked past them all, only ripping her glasses off and putting them into her short, blow-dried hair when her back was to them. "*Hurry*! I don't have all day!"

The rest of the choir lingered for a moment, looking like they didn't know if they wanted to follow or leave.

"Rita Bishop, I presume?" Julia asked Dot as they followed the unsure flock.

"Who else?"

Rita took her position at the front of the church, standing exactly where Father David had been during the ill-fated ceremony. Rita glanced at the spot where Gloria had fallen and died, but her eyes didn't linger for more than a second.

"Don't be *shy!*" Rita cried, a cold laugh leaving her red-tinted lips. "We have a lot to discuss, and, to perform here again, we'll need to get over what happened. We only have six days until Sunday's service, so chop-chop!"

Rita clapped her hands together as though summoning a pack of trained dogs. Julia held back and sat on the back pew with her gingerbread fireworks, not wanting to intrude any more than she already had.

The choir shuffled to the front of the church, taking seats on the front pews. Rita clasped her hands together and smiled down at them from her elevated position, looking ready to deliver a sermon.

"Firstly, I want to thank you all for coming," Rita started, her smile broadening as she looked at each of the members. Her eyes drifted up to Julia but didn't linger. "I wasn't sure you'd all be here considering the short notice, but it seems you're all as dedicated to saving this choir as I am."

Rita paused for breath. The other members shuffled in their seats, but none of them said anything.

"It's with great sadness that we meet here today." Rita again glanced at the spot where Gloria had died. "Gloria Gray served this choir for many decades and, for that, I think we're all grateful. A round of applause for Gloria!"

Rita clapped, but the other members joined in less enthusiastically. Julia squirmed in her seat, wondering if she was watching the world's most ill-timed performance art piece.

"That said, we cannot, and *will* not, linger in sadness!" Rita continued. "We are leaderless, and that can't be. Father David rightfully cancelled yesterday's service out of respect, but that just means we have six days to get ourselves together for this coming Sunday! So, going forward, I propose I take over Gloria's duties as choirmaster."

"It's only been two days!" Flora cried, jumping up from her seat. "You can't expect us to move on like that."

"It's what Gloria would have wanted." Rita snapped back with the frozen smile of a circus clown. "She loved this choir more than anything, and, despite our differences over the years, I'm not willing to let it go to rack and ruin, which is why I *selflessly* volunteer to take over the mammoth task of getting us performance-ready. If you think you'd make a better leader, Flora, by all means, stand up and take charge!"

Flora immediately sat down, her head bowing. Rita

didn't try to hide her pleasure at silencing the woman.

"We are on a sinking ship." Rita began to pace the stage. "You can all run like the rats or sit still and go down with the ship, but I intend to do *neither*! I propose we *change* things around here. No one person should perform all the solos. We should each have a chance to shine, and if you decide to elect me as your new choirmaster, I will make sure that we do that—not just in this church, but all over the country! Gloria always thought so *small*! There's a bigger audience out there for us. Choir is cool! There are competitions in every county, and, with a lot of work, we could be competing on a national scale."

"Gloria always said competitions weren't for real choirs," Flora piped up again. "Gloria said that we should—"

"Gloria is *dead*!" Rita cried, stopping in front of Flora. "If we stay in the past, we'll each die out one by one, and this choir will go with us! Members have been dropping like flies for years. Look at us! We're a pale imitation of what we once were. We need to evolve and grow if we want to survive in this modern age. I can help us do that. I have the passion it requires. If none of you wants me to take charge, I'll walk out that door and never return, but I think you crave the growth just as much as I do. We've all sat in these meetings, angry and upset at Gloria's narrow and selfish vision. She made herself a star while we all sang harmonies in the background. No more! We're all the stars of this choir, and I vow to show the world." Rita paused and inhaled deeply, regaining her spot in the centre, her hands clasped back together. "Raise your hand if you don't want me to be choirmaster."

No hands immediately floated up, which brought a grin to Rita's face. After almost a minute of silence, Flora's hand drifted shakily above her head.

"Only one?" Rita scanned the faces of the other members, daring them to object. "Just Flora? Then it's decided. I shall lead this choir into a new golden age. Flora, you can leave."

"*L-Leave?*"

"A group is only as strong as its weakest link." Rita planted her hands on her hips. "If you don't trust me, I can't trust you. Now, if you want to take back your vote, you're more than welcome, but if not, you know where the door is."

Rita swept her hand to the door as she smiled down at Flora. Flora stood up, clutching her baggy scarf. She looked around, wearing the same pitiful expression she'd had at Julia's cottage on the night of Gloria's death. Julia almost stood up and said something, but Skye beat her to the punch.

"This is *ridiculous!*" Skye cried, followed by a shaky laugh. "This is supposed to be *fun*. We're trading one dictator for another!"

"But we've wanted to do the competitions for years," Shilpa said. "If Rita can get us there, then—"

"We don't *need* Rita to get there." Skye tossed out her arms. "We can do it ourselves."

Rita marched off the step to draw level with Skye. Even though the young beauty was taller than Rita, the redhead's presence filled every corner of the room.

"Who here has an honours degree from the *Royal Academy of Music?*" Rita asked, raising her hand slowly above her head. "Only me?" She looked around and waited for another hand to raise, but none did. "I thought so. Do I need to say more?"

To Julia's surprise, Skye sat down. Nobody else sprang to Flora's defence. She wondered if being out of Gloria's shadow had left Flora without a place in the choir in the eyes of the other members. Flora stepped out of the pews and set off up the aisle, her eyes firmly on the floor. She passed Julia without looking up, and the door banged behind her when she left.

"You're free to follow, Skye." Rita motioned to the

door. "But I *know* you want the limelight more than anyone. You *crave* recognition for your voice, and you deserve it. You have natural talent, and you need training that I can give you. Gloria was content having you on the back row, but I won't be."

"But do we have to be so cruel about how we do things?"

"There's a difference between being *disciplined* and *cruel*," Rita said, her smile spreading again. "Stars are forged in the heart of an explosion, not in comfortable, quiet corners! Now, does anyone else have anything to say? I have to get to my Pilates class."

There was a general shaking of heads before Rita pulled her sunglasses from her hair and stormed down the aisle, her cardigan billowing behind her. The door slammed and seemed to send an icy shiver through the ancient building.

Julia watched as the other members continued to sit in silence. She couldn't believe they had all let Rita speak to them in such a way. She had never given the Peridale Harmonics Choir much thought. They popped up at small village events every now and then, but she had never considered how much they all craved something bigger. This desire had blinded them and allowed them to watch as Rita exiled Flora from the group. She looked down at her biscuits; the urge to share them had vanished.

With Rita gone, the rest of the members disbanded fairly quickly. Amy, Shilpa, and Evelyn were the first to leave, followed by Skye, with Alfie not far behind. Julia waited for Dot to get up, but she sensed she was lingering back to talk to Percy. Not wanting to intrude, Julia grabbed her box and headed to the vestibule.

While she waited, Father David walked in. She smiled at him and meant to ask if the wedding rings had turned up, but he walked into the church without acknowledging her.

"Odd."

The minutes ticked by as she waited for Dot to finish talking to Percy. She instinctively reached for her phone to check her messages, but she remembered she had left it at home. It felt nice to have lived without the distraction for a few days, but she wasn't sure she had the patience to be parted from it forever. When her foot started to tap, she decided to check in on her gran.

As she pulled the church door open, she nearly dropped her box of biscuits when she saw Dot holding hands with Percy. Percy leaned in and kissed Dot on the cheek, and she giggled like a lovesick teenager. Julia stepped back, a smile spreading across her face. Less than a minute later, the door opened, and Percy hurried out, nodding and smiling to Julia as he went. Dot followed seconds later, adjusting her brooch.

"Wasn't that *wild*?" Dot cried, linking arms with Julia. "It took all my energy to keep my mouth shut, but for the sake of being undercover, I let the woman rant on and on!"

Julia considered busting her gran's secret as they walked across the village green to Dot's cottage, but she bit her tongue.

"Wild," Julia replied, concealing her smile. "Very wild indeed."

6

"**W**edding Woe!'" Julia read the headline of *The Peridale Post's* latest front cover aloud. *"Really* Johnny? You put my botched wedding on the *front* page?"

"It's *newsworthy!"* Johnny blushed as he fiddled with his glasses. "And now that I'm the editor in chief of the paper, I need to make sure every issue grabs our readers' attention! They've promoted me because of my vision. I promised I would get readership up, and if I don't, goodbye paper. I can't be the guy who drops the ball after 132 years of circulation."

"But *Julia's* wedding?" Roxy clipped Johnny over the back of the head. "Our best friend, Julia? Couldn't you have gone with the singing cat on page six? I would have picked that up."

"Me too," Leah added, kissing Johnny on the cheek as she ruffled his hair. "You're outnumbered, Johnny. Bad move."

Even though Julia would rather her misfortune hadn't been spread across the front page, she knew Johnny was only doing his job, and news of the event would have spread to every corner of the village already. She couldn't be mad at him for using the situation to sell papers, especially after last week's less than tantalising 'Bus Shelter Vandalised! Whodunnit?' headline.

She tossed the paper onto the table and picked up her glass of wine. After sitting in on that morning's choir meeting, Julia had needed the company of her closest and oldest friends to throw their unfiltered opinions into the ring. She had always been able to count on Roxy and Johnny for their support, and after Leah's recent rocky return to the village, she'd regained her place in the group.

"I had no idea they took the choir so seriously," Leah said as she scanned The Plough's lunch menu. "I still keep forgetting how the most trivial things can become huge elephants in this village."

"They take it *very* seriously," Roxy said as she checked her teeth in the back of a spoon. "My mum was a member a couple of years ago. She joined to get out of the house and make some friends after my dad died, but she couldn't handle the pressure. She said the in-fighting and politics were worse than high school."

"Impossible," Johnny muttered under his breath. "Nothing is worse than high school."

"Well, according to my mother, that choir was." Roxy looked over Leah's shoulder at the menu. "I think I'm in the mood for a Christmas dinner. Is it too early?"

"It's never too early for Christmas." Leah passed the menu to Julia. "You've just made my mind up. I haven't had a Peridale Christmas dinner in years."

"I'll have the same," Johnny added as he flicked through the newspaper.

"Me too," Julia said.

"And that's why we're all the best of friends." Roxy slapped the table as she stood up. "I'll order. This one's on me. You two lovebirds bought last week's lunch, and

Julia, no offence, but you just wasted thousands on a wedding that didn't result in a marriage so you can keep your hand out of your pocket for a while."

Julia chuckled, grateful for Roxy's sense of humour in the bleak situation. She had worried her friends would offer their sympathy, but they hadn't treated her any differently, opting to make light of the tragedy, instead. She couldn't say the same for the other lunchtime diners, who were all burning holes in the back of her head. She was glad she had decided to sit facing the wall.

"This is the most exciting thing that's happened since I was kidnapped and chained up in that basement for a week," Leah said as she peered around the pub. "They've been ravenous for a new topic, and I think you might have just outdone my situation. Cheers for that."

"I'm glad to be of service." Julia lifted her glass and clinked it with Leah's. "Although, Roxy is right. I hadn't even thought about how much money we've wasted. The dress alone cost nearly a thousand."

"On a *dress*?" Johnny choked on his pint. "Are you *mad*?"

"No, she was a bride!" Leah pouted at Johnny. "I've had clients spend tens of thousands on dresses. Some even buy more than one! I had a client two years ago who bought four dresses because she couldn't decide. She kept changing during the reception, and then she threw a tantrum when nobody noticed. That was a long night."

"Who can be bothered?" Johnny rolled his eyes as he folded up the newspaper. "It seems like a lot of effort for a party."

"It's not a party!" Leah shook her head as she forced out a laugh. "*Men*! It's one of the most important days of your life. Why do you think people put so much effort in? If they didn't, I'd be out of a job."

"I think Johnny might be onto something." Julia glanced at her engagement ring. "I was so sure I wanted to emulate my mother's wedding, and then none it went the way I wanted. I thought I'd gone simple and small, but there were so many moving parts. I could have been stood there in a potato sack, and I still would have wanted to marry Barker. When we didn't, none of the other stuff mattered. It felt so trivial."

Roxy returned to the table and sat down. "What are we talking about?"

"Weddings," Julia said, circling her glass with a fingertip. "Do you think they're worth it?"

"I couldn't be bothered." Roxy shrugged. "All that fuss for one day? No, thanks."

"Thank you!" Johnny exclaimed, slapping his hand on the table. "Roxy gets it!"

"But what about Violet?" Leah urged. "Don't you love her?"

"More than anything."

"Then why don't you want to marry her?"

"I never said I didn't *want* to," Roxy fired back, "but *if* I do, the wedding itself isn't that important to me. I wasn't one of those little girls who dreamed of having a fairy-tale wedding, mainly because I imagined my Prince Charming as *Princess* Charming. If the time felt right, I wouldn't make any fuss."

"And how does Violet feel about that?" Leah asked.

"She's Russian." Roxy sipped from her pint. "She's not big on grand gestures of emotion. As long as there's vodka and pirozhki, she's set for the day."

Leah sighed and relaxed into her chair. Despite having two divorces under her belt and having vowed never to marry again, Leah looked upset that the conversation had taken such a turn. Julia wondered if it was because Leah was a wedding planner, or because she had fallen head over heels in love with Johnny and wanted to marry him.

"What happened to romance?" Leah asked, tossing

her hair over her shoulder. "That huge day to celebrate the beginning of your life together is supposed to be special. Start with a bang?"

"My idea of romance is when Violet rubs my feet after I've been stood up at school teaching six-year-olds all day." Roxy took another swig of her pint. "Which I'd be doing right now, so cheers to that burst pipe in the boys' toilets!"

The conversation shifted from weddings to Christmas, and then back to Julia's wedding again when their food came out. When they were halfway through eating their turkey, stuffing, and brussels sprouts, the topic veered to Gloria's sudden death.

"It has to be Rita," Leah mumbled through a mouthful of roast potato. "If her speech was as vibrant as you described it, there's no other explanation. She somehow killed Gloria to ascend to the throne."

"How did she even kill her?" Roxy asked. "Mind control? Poor woman dropped like a house. She didn't stand a chance."

"Maybe it was natural causes?" Johnny suggested. "She was overweight. Maybe her heart just gave out? She was singing quite loud."

"That's hardly going to sell your papers, is it?" Roxy rolled her eyes. "Stop the press! 'Woman Dies of

Natural Causes!'"

"It's just an idea." Johnny blushed as he shovelled more turkey into his mouth. "Have the police confirmed that it was murder?"

"As good as," Julia replied, "and don't you dare quote me on that, editor!"

"What do you think happened to her, Julia?" Leah asked.

Before Julia could answer, her phone vibrated in her bag, which she had collected on the way to the pub. Having gone so long without it, it took her by surprise and made her jump in her seat. She was relieved to see it was a text message from Barker.

"Arsenic poisoning," she said.

"Oh, c'mon!" Roxy chuckled as she sawed through a tough piece of turkey skin. "Isn't that all a little 'wife killing off her husband so she can run off with the butler in 1856'?"

"No, really." Julia held up her phone to show the message from Barker. "Official confirmation from the toxicology report. DI Christie just told Barker."

They silently stared at the phone for a moment, their knives and forks hovering over their food.

"How does someone even get poisoned by arsenic?" Leah asked before popping a sprout into her mouth.

"Well, for a start, it's tasteless, odourless, and colourless." Julia tucked her phone away. "It's not easy to get hold of, but it's not impossible. It naturally occurs in nature, and it just so happens to be our natural Kryptonite. Rice even has small traces of it, though not enough to kill us. Slip a little of the pure stuff into someone's drink, or even their food, and they're not likely to live to tell the tale."

Leah spat out the sprout and dropped her knife and fork. Johnny and Roxy did the same, pushing their plates away from them.

"And suddenly I've lost my appetite," Roxy said with a sigh before patting her stomach. "Probably for the best. I've been using ''tis the season' since October to keep stuffing my face."

"Arsenic poisoning?" Johnny echoed, shifting in his seat. "That's a very intentional way to kill someone."

"There goes your natural causes theory," Leah said, tapping him on the knee. "Whoever killed Gloria really meant to do it."

"She could have ingested it by accident," Julia suggested. "But that doesn't seem likely."

They reflected in silence for another minute. Shirley, the landlady, came over and cleared away their half-finished dinners. Julia sipped her wine and leaned back in her chair, mind whirring.

"Why your wedding?" Leah asked.

"Huh?"

"Why kill her during your wedding?" Leah repeated, sitting up straight. "If someone meant to kill her, they could have poisoned her at any time. And why poison? They could have killed her all kinds of ways."

"Maybe they wanted to send a message?" Julia suggested. "To me? To the village? To Gloria during her last minutes alive?"

"Or they were in a rush." Roxy finished her pint and rose, grabbing her jacket from the back of her chair. "Speaking of which, I should get going. I promised Violet we'd clean out the spare room since we have the day off school. She wants to turn it into a crafting room. We watched *Ghost* last week, and she's convinced she's going to start pottery."

"Are you Patrick Swayze or Demi Moore?" Johnny asked.

"Oh, Swayze all day long." Roxy winked. "Don't call. I'm sick and tired of the lot of you."

"Love you too," Julia said as Roxy kissed her on the cheek. "Be good."

"Shan't." Roxy waved as she headed for the door.

"I'll see you losers around."

"Will we see you at the bonfire tonight?" Leah called before Roxy left. "I heard they've gone all out with the fireworks."

"Fireworks?" Roxy thought about it for a second. "I'll pass. I think I'd rather clean my spare room, to be honest. See-ya!"

"And just like that, we're sixteen again," Johnny said with a fiddle of his glasses. "Who said we have to age gracefully?"

"Forty is the new twenty, according to a magazine I read in the doctor's waiting room," Leah said after finishing her wine. "And beige is going to be a big trend for spring and summer next year, which is going to make my wedding portfolio as exciting as a bowl of porridge." She patted Johnny on the shoulder and stood up. "We should get going too. I'm pitching my ideas to a fussy bride in an hour, and you've got that piece about the stolen street signs to research."

"Ever the exciting life." Johnny drained his pint before standing up and pulling his messenger bag across his body. "Good luck with your mystery, Julia."

"Will we see *you* at the bonfire?" Leah asked. "There'll be treacle toffee."

"As tempting as destroying my teeth on toffee

sounds, I think I'm going to pass too." Julia smiled. "I'm not quite ready to face the world on that scale yet."

"I understand." Leah ruffled Julia's hair before kissing her on the cheek. "If you change your mind, I'm leaving my cottage at seven."

"Can I credit you as a source regarding the arsenic poisoning revelation?" Johnny asked. "It's important that the people know what's going on."

"Nope."

"Worth a try."

Johnny and Leah left arm in arm, leaving Julia alone in the pub. She reached into her handbag and pulled out her small notepad. It was open on her working sketch of her wedding cake design. She ripped out the page and scrunched it up before dropping it into her bag. On a fresh page, she wrote 'Gloria Gray' in the middle, with 'arsenic poisoning' underneath. Beneath that, she wrote 'Motive: message or necessity?', underlining both. She enclosed the entire thing in a bubble and drew two lines away and wrote her two suspects. On one tangent, she wrote 'Rita Bishop: Rival Leader', and 'Skye (surname???): Denied Lead Vocals', on the other.

It wasn't a lot to work on, but it was a start. She knew the police might be interviewing suspects even as she scribbled her notes, but the conundrum gave her something to occupy her mind. Without her friends distracting her, it was easy to slip into her own dark thoughts.

She was about to pocket her notepad when another thought sprang to mind. She turned to a fresh page. With her pen hovering over the paper, she hesitated before writing 'Father David' in the middle. She drew a giant '?' through his name, and then added 'blanked me like a stranger' underneath. He had probably been deep in his thoughts, especially after having witnessed his choirmaster die during one of his wedding ceremonies, but a niggling feeling in the back of her mind wanted to investigate further.

Satisfied she had exhausted all she knew so far, she finished the last drop of wine and dropped her pad back into her bag. When she stood up, the picture of Gloria Gray on the front page of Johnny's abandoned *The Peridale Post* stared up at her.

"Who would want to kill you?" Julia whispered to the picture. "Who did you upset, Gloria?"

7

Even though Julia had decided against going to the village's annual bonfire, Barker convinced her it would be a good idea to get out and face the world before reopening her café, if only to show everyone she was still standing. With Jessie on a date with Billy to catch the last showing of a horror movie left over from Halloween, Julia didn't want to spend a silent night alone in the house while Barker wrote in the dining room. They wrapped up in hats, scarves, gloves, and heavy coats, and met Leah outside her cottage across the lane a little before seven.

"I'm so glad you decided to come," Leah said, her breath turning to steam as they walked arm in arm down the dark lane, fireworks popping in the sky all over the village. "I haven't seen a bonfire as big as Peridale's in over twenty years. I never realised how much I missed the little things about village life."

They waited a couple of minutes at the bottom of the lane before Johnny joined them. Following the scent of burning wood, they crossed the village green and started towards St. Peter's Primary School. They veered off halfway, climbing over the wall and into the field between the school and the graveyard.

The bonfire, which was held in the same spot on the edge of Haworth Forest every year, stood as tall and wide as a two-story house. It burned bright in the dark, orange sparks crackling up to the inky sky.

They ventured into the sea of villagers who had come out to witness the tradition. Children held out fizzing sparklers, and their parents ate jacket potatoes that had been cooked in the fire. As was custom, Guy Fawkes' giant effigy burned brightly at the top of the blaze. Even from a hundred feet away, the heat from the fire was something to behold.

"There you losers are!" a familiar voice called from behind them. "I've been looking for you everywhere."

Roxy and Violet, both wrapped-up in thick woolly layers, appeared behind them. Violet was licking a treacle lollypop, her eyes firmly fixed on the giant furnace.

"I thought this wasn't your scene?" Leah asked.

"Violet wanted to come and see it." Roxy rolled her eyes as she nodded at her girlfriend. "We were on holiday this time last year. The whole concept of Bonfire Night boggles her mind."

"You celebrate ancient terrorist who tried to blow up your government building!" Violet cried in her thick accent, a grin spreading across her pale, beautiful face. "If I did not know better, I'd think this was Russian tradition!"

"We don't celebrate *him*, as such," Barker said, shivering as he stuffed his hands into his pockets. "And he wasn't just one man; he was part of a group of eight Catholic men who wanted to blow up the Houses of Parliament to assassinate King James The First, who was a Protestant. It was an act of treason."

"So, they wanted to shoot the king?" Violet asked, still mesmerised by the fire. "With thirty-six guns?"

"Thirty-six barrels of gun*powder*," Barker corrected her. "They had been stored under Parliament, and the assassins wanted to set them on fire when they knew the king was going to be there. Think a 1605 version of a giant bomb. It wasn't even Guy Fawkes' idea, but he was the gunpowder expert and the guy who was caught red-handed before they had the chance to blow anything up. Bonfires started all over the country as a celebration that the king was alive. The following year, it became an official public day of thanksgiving, and we've kept it up for four hundred years. I don't really know why, it's just something we do."

"It's an excuse to build a giant fire and set off fireworks," Roxy said. "Who knew you were such a geek?"

"He's not just a pretty face." Julia mushed his cheeks with her hands. "Brains, too."

"I love your silly British traditions," Violet chuckled as she looked down at her lollypop. "But treacle toffee tastes like old feet."

They basked in the warmth of the fire while Barker spent the next fifteen minutes talking about how the entire country would have been very different if the Gunpowder Plot had succeeded. Julia's interest in history was limited but seeing Barker's face light up as he spoke warmed her more than the fire. Even though Roxy and Leah kept letting out yawns, Johnny and Violet listened to every word.

Julia tried to follow along, but her mind wandered, as did her eyes. She scanned the familiar faces in the crowd. People smiled and nodded at her, and even though she received a few questionable expressions, being in public wasn't as bad as she had expected. She felt safe behind her many layers of clothing, with her fiancé and friends to accompany her.

She glanced at the jacket potato stall and let out a yawn; a moment later, she heard a man shouting. She almost paid it no attention, until she saw that the shouting man was gripping a tiny woman's arm. Even though Julia could only see the back of the woman's wiry hair and long coat, she recognised Flora.

"I'll grab us some potatoes," Julia said as she broke away. "I won't be long."

She weaved through the crowd and reached the stall just as Flora broke away from the man's grip. She bumped into Julia and fell back onto the ground, a foil-wrapped potato falling out of her hand and rolling onto the grass.

"Is everything okay here?" Julia asked as she helped Flora up.

"No, it's *not!*" the man cried, his face turning bright red. He snatched up the potato. "That old biddy just tried nicking one of my spuds!"

"I thought they were free," Flora muttered, her eyes on the ground. "I didn't know."

"Can't you read the sign?" The man jabbed his finger on a piece of cardboard. "£1.99 per spud, or three for £5. There's no five-finger discount here!"

Julia rested her hand on Flora's arm as she looked down at her. From the way Flora was avoiding her gaze, Julia knew she had tried to steal the potato, but she wasn't going to hand Flora to the wolves; like Julia, she had been through enough.

"I'm sure it was an honest mistake." Julia gave the man a stern look. "Now, if you don't mind, I'll take seven jacket potatoes, please."

The man scowled at Flora, but he reluctantly loaded the bonfire-cooked spuds with butter. Julia handed over the money, and he passed over the food. With Flora's help, they walked back to the group and handed them out.

"You remember Flora, don't you, Barker?" Julia said, ushering Flora into the group.

"Five sugars," Barker nodded. "Nice to see you again."

Flora smiled but barely looked up at the group. They all watched, jaws agape, as she devoured her potato as though she hadn't eaten in months.

"Thank you," Flora said, wiping her buttery lips with the back of her fingerless-gloved hand. "I won't intrude."

Flora turned and scurried away, but Julia wasn't about to let her leave without an explanation. She handed her potato to Barker and ran after the tiny, nimble woman, taking them around the fire and towards the edge of Haworth Forest.

"*Flora!*" Julia cried. "Wait!"

Flora stopped in her tracks and glanced over her shoulder. She looked as though she wanted to continue her escape, but she turned and walked up to Julia instead.

"Is everything okay?" Julia asked softly. "What happened back there at the potato stall?"

"I didn't see the sign," Flora mumbled. "Like you said, honest mistake."

Julia sighed, but she knew she wasn't going to get a truthful answer from the strange lady. She wanted to know why someone in their seventies would need to steal food, but she didn't want to offend her. It looked like it wouldn't take a lot to push her over the edge.

"I've wanted to talk to you about what happened at the meeting this morning," Julia started. "I'm really sorry that happened to you. It mustn't have been nice."

"I was going to quit anyway." Flora shrugged before wiping her glistening nose with her glove. "It was never going to be the same without Gloria. None of them liked me, because I liked Gloria."

"I wanted to ask you more about her," Julia said, glad the dead choirmaster had come up in conversation. "I don't really know anything about her, aside from her role in the choir and that she used to be a music teacher at the primary school."

"Gloria never liked children." Flora pursed her lips. "She always said they were the spawn of the devil. I think that's why she never had any. It didn't mean she didn't have a big heart, though. She did, but in other ways. She always looked after me."

"How so?"

"Little ways." Flora shrugged, as though not wanting to reveal the intricacies of their relationship. "She was an only child, and her parents died years ago, so it was just her and me. We met in the post office in 1983. I was short a penny for a bottle of milk, and she made up the difference. Not many people would do that, you know? She told me about the choir, so I joined. I didn't care about the singing, I just liked having her as a friend. I didn't have any friends growing up. The kids at school called me Freaky Flora. Gloria was right about children. They're so cruel. She was never cruel to me. It wasn't her fault that the other choir members were jealous of her."

"Don't you have any family?" Julia asked, her heart breaking. "Brothers and sisters?"

"A brother. Timothy. We're not close. My father died when we were little, and my mother couldn't cope. They sent her to the nut house. They didn't treat you right back then. They didn't help you; they pumped you full of pills and zapped your brain. She was never the same after that. I woke up one morning, and she just wasn't there. I think Timothy blamed me because I was the older one. We haven't spoken in years. It's just been Gloria and me. She was all I needed. She was my family, and now she's gone, and it's all my fault!"

Flora covered her face with her gloves and began to sob. Julia knew Flora didn't like being touched, but she couldn't help herself. She pulled Flora into a hug.

"Why's it your fault?" she asked when Flora finally stopped crying.

"I should have known something like this would happen," Flora blubbered. "I should have protected her like she protected me for all those years. In her hour of need, all I could do was stand by and watch her die."

"There was nothing any of us could have done," Julia reassured her. "Can you think of any other reason anyone would want to kill Gloria? Did she have any connections or history with the other members?"

Flora thought for a minute as she wiped away her tears.

"There's Percy," she said. "She and Percy had a thing about a decade ago. It didn't go anywhere. It fizzled out before it really started. I think him being so much older than she put her off."

"Percy Cropper?"

"They met at a magic show," Flora explained. "Percy used to put on shows. He wasn't very good, but Gloria thought he was funny. He charmed her. They only went on a couple of dates. She said he never put his hand in his pocket to pay for anything. She assumed he was using her."

As Julia's thoughts turned to Percy, the fireworks display began with a giant rocket exploding in the sky behind her. The bang made her jump, and she spun around to look up as red sparks scattered across the black canvas above. She watched two more fireworks pop and fizzle. When she turned back to Flora, she was gone.

Julia scanned the motionless, observing crowd, but she couldn't see the tiny woman anywhere. She even looked at the edge of the forest, but the darkness claimed everything beyond the first row of trees.

"There you are!" Barker called to Julia when she returned, his eyes still firmly on the sky. "Where've you been?"

"Talking to Flora," Julia said as she continued to look around the crowd. "She just vanished."

"Well, she is a little freaky," Barker said.

"Don't say that." A lump rose in Julia's throat. "She's harmless."

She looped her arm through Barker's and watched the impressive display. A never-ending stream of fireworks of every colour and size erupted above the village, the bangs echoing for miles around. After the last impressive shower of colour, the crowd applauded and cheered. From memory, Julia knew the festivities continued late into the night, with the teenagers and young adults sticking around until the early hours. It was something she had done with Roxy, Johnny, and Leah in their youth, but she wasn't about to replay that old tape tonight.

After saying their goodbyes, Julia and Barker

hopped over the wall and walked back down the lane hand in hand. She wanted nothing more than to go home, get into her pyjamas, and relax, even if her mind was still firmly fixed on Gloria and everything Flora had told her. She almost talked it through with Barker, but she held back, deciding that she wanted to talk to Percy to get a different perspective on Gloria's life.

"Thank you for getting me out tonight," Julia said when they were unravelling their layers back at their warm cottage. "Only a couple of people looked at me like I had two heads."

"They have short memories around here," Barker assured her. "They'll forget all about it when the next thing comes along. And then we can have another wedding, and everything will be as it should."

"You still want another wedding?"

"Don't you?"

"After how the last one turned out," Julia said as she kicked off her shoes, "it feels like tempting fate to go through that again."

"Lightning doesn't strike twice in the same place." Barker helped her out of her coat and hung it up on the hat stand beside his. "Everything will be fine."

Julia smiled and nodded, even though she felt far from fine. Barker shut himself in the dining room to reply to work emails, leaving Julia to retreat to the sitting room with her notepad. Mowgli curled up on her lap as she scribbled down everything Flora had told her about Gloria on a fresh page. None of it felt important, but she didn't want to dismiss any information, considering how little she had to work with.

Flipping back to her list of suspects, she added: "Percy Cropper: Former Love Interest" next to Rita and Skye without thinking twice about it. It felt like a betrayal against her gran, but she knew very little about the man who was stealing her gran's heart. Before she discounted him, she needed to talk to him and find out what he knew.

As she stared at her notes, she realised she had yet to talk to Skye. She glanced at her phone and considered texting Alfie to ask if he'd found anything out, but Mowgli was comfortable, and she didn't want to disrupt him.

Instead, she picked up the remote from the chair arm and turned on the television, which was playing an episode of a baking competition show. Watching the bakers sweat over their creations made her realise how much she was missing her café, but before she could dwell on it for too long, her eyelids fluttered, and her mind slipped away.

Agatha Frost

8

"Are you sure you don't want to do something bigger for your birthday?" Julia asked as she fastened Barker's tie in their bedroom the next night. "You don't turn forty every day."

"After the surprise party you threw me last year and everything that has happened so far this week, I'm more than happy having a quiet meal at The Comfy Corner." Barker stepped back and assessed his shirt and tie in the mirror. "Why did Jessie have to buy me a pink shirt?"

"She knew you'd wear it because you care about her." Julia dusted along his shoulders. "And teenagers are mean like that."

"Do I look silly?"

She tilted her head and took the vibrant colour in.

"No."

"Does it suit me?"

She tilted her head again.

"No."

"I much prefer your present." He tugged at the tight collar as though he feared the shirt was growing into his skin. "A box of monogrammed, leather-bound notepads is a writer's dream. I might need them to scrap and restart my second novel if the publishers hate what I handed in last week. I worked my backside off finishing that first draft, and they haven't made a peep."

"When do I get to read it?" Julia fixed her diamond studs in her ears. "Or find out what it's about, for that matter?"

"When I'm sure it isn't entirely awful." Barker sighed as he fiddled with his waxed hair in the mirror. "So, never?"

"I'm sure it's perfect. If it's anything like your first book, it's going to be another runaway smash." Julia tiptoed and kissed him on the cheek. "Now, enough doubt for today. It's your birthday!"

"Doubt and worry seem to be my permanent setting since I ditched the police force and dove into writing fulltime." Barker spritzed aftershave on his neck before helping Julia with her necklace. "Although, I don't envy DI Christie with this case. Arsenic poisoning is nasty business. It's almost impossible to trace because it's so hard to buy. Unless they stumble on a signed confession, they're going to have a tough time proving how she was fed the lethal dose."

They slipped into their shoes and joined Jessie, who was waiting by the door, her face buried in her phone. She wore high-waisted blue jeans with a baggy black band t-shirt tucked in. A short, studded leather jacket and wedged heel boots completed the outfit. It was a simple look she had worn more than once, but seeing her waiting by the door, a handbag slung over her shoulder, made her look so grown-up.

"What are you looking at, cake lady?" Jessie asked without glancing away from her phone. "I can feel your beady eyes staring at me."

"I just think you look pretty, that's all," Julia said as she reached around Jessie to grab her pink pea coat from the hat stand. "Or is that not allowed?"

"Whatever." Jessie pushed her phone into her pocket and grabbed her keys from the dish on the side table. "I'll drive. That way, you can both have a drink."

"I thought you'd want to have a drink, being the eighteen-year-old." Barker brushed down his shirt. "We could head to a rave after the meal and show off my new shirt. I have a theory that if it gets under a black light, it's going to glow like a neon sign."

"When did you get so uncool, Barker?" Jessie rolled her eyes.

"About sixteen hours ago when I ceased to be in my thirties?" he said after checking his watch. "But thanks to your excellent fashion pick, people will see me coming through a fog on a dark night. That's pretty cool, right?"

Jessie laughed and shook her head as she opened the door. She shooed them out into the night before locking the cottage behind them. They climbed into Jessie's yellow Mini Cooper, which had been a gift from Barker for Jessie's eighteenth birthday.

Julia was rarely a passenger in Jessie's car. Not because Jessie didn't like driving, but because Jessie loved driving a little too much, and Julia never felt quite safe. No matter how many times Jessie insisted she had passed her test, her knowledge of clutch control, gears, and breaking seemed to contradict the result. Julia and Barker speculated that the driving school only passed Jessie because it was her eighth attempt and they were sick and tired of seeing her.

"Just *ease* it in!" Barker cried as they attempted to manoeuvre into a space outside The Comfy Corner. "I said, *ease*! Are you in first?"

"*No!*" Jessie cried. "Third!"

"Why are you trying to park in *third*?" Barker yelled back, almost throwing himself into the front seat. "*First!* You always park in *first*!"

"I know!" Jessie yanked the gear stick. "Why won't it move?"

"*Clutch!*"

"Right." Jessie put her foot down and put the car into first. "You're stressing me out! I can do it fine when I'm on my own!"

The car jerked like a rollercoaster as Jessie attempted to fit her Mini into a space that would have been fine for a double-decker bus. She pulled up in the middle of the space in a diagonal line, and instead of straightening it up, she put it into neutral, yanked up the handbrake, and killed the engine. Barker looked like he was going to say something, so Julia rested her hand on his knee and shook her head. Leaving the car where

Jessie had decided it belonged, they walked into the restaurant.

The Comfy Corner was the only place in Peridale that deserved to be called a real restaurant. The pub served food, as did Julia's café during the day, but nowhere else had the homely atmosphere that the owners, Mary and Todd Porter, had created here. Newcomers often likened it to walking into an old friend's home, which Julia had always thought was an apt description. It was also common knowledge in the village that The Comfy Corner had the best food in Peridale, if not the whole of the Cotswolds.

"*Julia!*" Mary greeted her with open arms. "You *poor* dear! Come here. Let me hug you."

Mary was a curvy woman in her sixties, and, if gossiping were a sport, she would take the gold medal. Nothing got past her, and if you wanted somewhere to have a private conversation, you knew to stay away from The Comfy Corner. Despite being a one-woman rumour mill, she had a heart of gold and would give people the clothes off her back if they asked. She had known her husband, Todd, since childhood, and theirs was often the standard that most relationships in the village were compared to.

"I wanted to rush right over the moment I heard!"

Mary pulled Julia in even tighter. "But you know I don't get away from this place that often. It's my baby. I did try to call, but the line was dead. Perhaps I have the wrong number?"

"We've had issues with the line," Barker lied. "It should be fixed now."

"Well, if there's anything I can do for you, say the word." Mary pulled away and cupped Julia's face in her hands. "How about a bottle of wine on the house? The rest of your party are in the snug. I'll bring through the bottle with some glasses."

Leaving them to find their table, Mary scurried off to the bar. The restaurant had been a tavern centuries ago, and the snug was a separate room thought to have been a games room. Now, it was where Mary seated parties for privacy away from the rest of the restaurant. Casper and Heather were already seated at one end of the table, deep in conversation.

"Ah, here he is!" Heather clapped her hands together, startling Casper and making him spill a portion of his pint down his front. "The birthday boy! Finally forty! How do you feel?"

"The same." Barker accepted a hug from Heather. "Should I feel different?"

"You will!" Heather cried as she took her seat. "I

117

adored my forties. They were some of the best years of my life. I really came into being who I am. You spend your twenties lost, your thirties figuring yourself out, and your forties enjoying what you figured out in your thirties. And when you get there, you're probably going to have a near mental breakdown when you reach your fifties, like your brother did." Heather nodded at Casper. "But, in your sixties, life will slow down to a lovely pace. We're both about to enter our seventies, so, in ten years, I'll let you know how that goes."

Casper half-stood up, using the table for support. He stared at Barker with narrowed eyes before jiggling his moustache.

"New shirt?" he asked, arching a brow.

"Birthday present off Jessie," Barker explained, blushing as pink as his shirt. "I'm still trying to figure out how to wear it."

Jessie gave a small snort while Casper grunted disapprovingly. They all took their seats around the table, with Julia choosing a seat with a view through the door to the rest of the restaurant. She noticed Mary hurrying around the bar with a stack of menus under one arm and a bottle of wine in her other hand.

"There you go!" She placed the wine in the middle of the table before passing out the menus. "We debuted our new festive menu yesterday, so feel free to dig in! I'd recommend the pigs in blankets pie or the turkey stuffing roast, but you can't go wrong with anything my Todd is cooking. I'll be back in a moment to take your orders."

Julia stared blankly at the menu, but her mind was somewhere else entirely. She was thinking about one thing, and one thing only: arsenic. She had spent the whole day doing as much research as possible on the poison, and all she had concluded was that anyone could have slipped Gloria the lethal dose at any point on the morning of the wedding.

"I like the sound of the pigs in blankets pie," Barker said to Julia, breaking her from her thoughts. "What are you getting?"

"Same." She put the menu down and pushed forward a smile. "Sounds good to me."

While Heather and Casper chatted about their plans for a holiday in the new year, Julia drifted back into her thoughts. She wished they had invited a couple more people so her mental absence wouldn't be as noticeable. She tried her best to smile and nod when there were natural pauses in the conversation.

"This is on me," Barker announced, "so order whatever you want. I'm getting my second royalty payment next week."

"I really did enjoy your book, Barker," Heather said as she scanned the menu. "I couldn't believe you wrote it! And I mean that with love because it was very good! We talked about it in our book club. I didn't mention that you were my brother-in-law until after we'd discussed it."

"And?"

"Everyone loved it!" Heather exclaimed. "Even you read it, didn't you, Casper?"

"It was my bathroom book," he explained before sipping his pint. "You know I like to take my time."

Mary entered the snug and made her way around the table to take orders. When she was finished, Julia's mind slipped away again, this time back to her wedding day. She drifted away so much that when she reached out for her glass of wine, she missed completely, the side of her hand grazing against the damp glass. The cold sensation shocked her, and she jerked her hand, sending the glass flying at Barker. The white wine splashed against his pink shirt, darkening the fabric.

"*Oh my!*" Julia cried as she reached for her napkin. "I'm so sorry!"

Jessie snickered under her breath as Julia flapped at the stain with a tissue.

"It's fine." Barker rested his hand on hers and dabbed at it with his napkin. "You've somehow made it even pinker. I think I'll need to dry it in the bathroom. I'll be right back."

Barker excused himself from the table, leaving Julia to finish mopping up the spilt wine. Her cheeks heated at her clumsy mistake. She hoped they hadn't noticed how far away she had been from their conversation.

"Any luck finding the rings?" Heather asked quietly, leaning across the table. "I didn't want to ask in front of Barker in case it hit a nerve again."

"For the *last* time, *I* didn't *lose* them!" Casper announced. "They were in my pocket, and then they weren't. I had nothing to do with it!"

"I know, I know." Heather patted him on the shoulder. "Julia?"

"Nothing yet." She screwed up the napkins and placed them on the end of the table. "I was at the church yesterday morning. I meant to ask Father David, but he seemed lost in a world of his own."

"They'll turn up when you least expect it," Heather said with a definite nod, "and in the place you least expect. Life has a funny way of working like that."

Barker returned from the bathroom, his shirt somewhat dryer, but still stained. From the determined look on his face, Julia could tell he had something to tell her.

"You'll *never* guess who I just saw in lover's corner," Barker whispered to her. "You said Rita Bishop had red curly hair, wore black turtlenecks, and was about forty-five?"

"I did."

"Then I think she's here on a date with a man at least half her age." Barker pulled himself under the table and poured himself a fresh glass of wine. "I recognised him from somewhere, but I can't put my finger on it."

"Oh."

"If you're going to have a look, you might want to hurry." Barker glanced through the door and nodded at Mary. "I think they just asked for the bill."

Julia watched as Mary punched some numbers into a calculator before scribbling on a piece of paper and slipping it into a leather wallet. Excusing herself from the table, Julia left the snug and followed behind Mary as she walked towards lover's corner, where she always seated people she thought were on dates.

When Julia spotted the back of Rita's head, she was surprised Barker had recognised her from her description. She was dressed as lavishly as she had been during the emergency choir meeting the day before, this time with a black fur shawl replacing the cardigan. The man she was with had white blond hair and fair skin and couldn't have been any older than twenty-five. It took Julia a second to realise where she recognised him from.

While the man settled the bill, Rita pushed away from the table and walked towards the lady's bathroom. Julia waited for a moment before following. She lingered by the sinks while Rita locked herself in a stall. When the toilet flushed, Julia turned on the tap and washed her hands.

The stall door opened, and Rita sauntered out with as much confidence and arrogance as she had radiated at the church. She positioned herself at the sink next to Julia and stared ahead at her reflection without giving Julia so much as a second glance. After washing her hands, Rita flicked the water from them, not seeming to care that she splashed Julia's arms. She dragged two blue paper towels from the dispenser, dried her hands, and dropped the towels on the floor.

"Rita?" Julia called before the woman left the bathroom. "From the choir?"

"Yes?" Rita stared down at Julia, her red lipstick twisted into somewhat of a smile. "Can I help you?"

"I was at the meeting yesterday." Julia grabbed a

paper towel and dried her hands. "My gran is a member. Dot?"

"Ah, yes." Rita nodded, arching a brow. "The new oldie. She can't sing a lick, but she's making up the numbers. The young fella she comes with has a fantastic voice though. I can't wait to work with him. Alan, or something?"

"Alfie," Julia corrected her. "He's my daughter's brother."

"So, your son?"

"She's adopted," Julia explained. "There's only a decade between Alfie and me."

"Interesting." Rita looked Julia up and down. "How modern. You look older. Your dress looks like it was pulled from an old war movie. Bizarre. Very bizarre, indeed."

Julia could have said many things about Rita's over-the-top outfit, but she bit her tongue. She wondered if the new choirmaster ever spoke without ladling out insults to everyone she encountered.

"I'm sorry about your friend's death," Julia said, choosing her words carefully.

"My *friend*?"

"Gloria."

"Right." Rita chuckled as she shifted her weight on

her feet. "I wouldn't exactly have called her a *friend*, but that's life, isn't it? You live, you die, the end."

"I heard she was murdered."

"She was?" Rita fanned a yawn out of her mouth as she checked her watch. "Is this going anywhere, dear?"

"It was during my wedding. You probably don't recognise me in this ... *bizarre* dress."

"That was *you*?" Rita looked Julia up and down again and tittered. "You certainly scrubbed up well, didn't you? You look like an entirely different person. Shame it ended the way it did. Is there a point to this little chat?"

Julia inhaled deeply, not wanting to rise to Rita's bait. Did anyone ever dare to challenge the sizzling redhead about her attitude?

"Do you have any idea who would have wanted to kill Gloria?" Julia asked, folding her arms. "I heard it was one of the choir members."

"You heard that, did you?" Rita rolled her eyes before narrowing them on Julia. "What did you say you did for a living?"

"I didn't. I run the café in the village."

"Oh, that little place." Rita cocked her head to the side. "Bless you. I've never been in. Doesn't look like my sort of establishment. Why are you so interested in

Gloria's death?"

"I'm just curious," she lied.

Rita seemed to consider her thoughts for a moment, a smirk pricking up the corners of her lips. She shrugged, raising her brows as her smirk broke free.

"I *will* say this." Rita turned to the mirror and fluffed up her hair before turning and pulling on the door. "These things have a habit of coming out when the dirty laundry is aired, and I shouldn't think it will take too long for that to happen. Now, if you'll excuse me, my son will be waiting for me."

Rita left the bathroom. Julia screwed up her paper towels and tossed them into the bin before picking up the ones Rita had discarded on the floor. She turned to the mirror and stared at her 1940s-inspired teal dress.

"It's not bizarre," she said to herself with a firm nod. "I like it."

She hurried back to her table. The food had been brought out, and everyone had already tucked in. Julia shuffled under the table and picked up her knife and fork.

"The blond guy she was with was Alec Bishop," Julia whispered to Barker as she sliced into her pie. "He was the photographer and videographer we hired for the wedding."

"*That's* where I know him from!" Barker snapped his fingers. "He was floating around the B&B all morning taking pictures of everything. Did Rita give you anything?"

"I think she knows what happened to Gloria." Julia wrinkled her nose as she replayed what Rita had said. "She made some weirdly-worded comment about dirty laundry being aired when I asked if she knew who would have wanted to kill Gloria."

"Dirty laundry? What do you think she means by that?"

"I don't know. Something." Julia lifted the first mouthful of food to her lips, but she paused. "I need to figure out what she knows, and I have a feeling she isn't the kind of lady who likes to share."

"Maybe you could go through her son?" Barker mumbled through a mouthful of pie. "He might be easier to get through."

"Was he at the wedding?"

"Yep," Jessie butted in, leaning across the table. "I saw him at the side. He was taking pictures the whole time. You know you're not whispering, right? I can hear every word you're saying."

Deciding to leave the topic until later, Julia tucked into her pie and focused on the meal at hand. They drained the free bottle of wine and ordered a second, and then a third. A birthday cake Julia had given to Heather to bring came out at the end, with forty candles decorating the top. Barker blew them out and then cut into the double chocolate fudge cake, which he proclaimed was the best she had ever made.

After paying the bill, they left the restaurant at nine. Casper and Heather were ready to leave Peridale and drive back home in their bright orange Volkswagen camper van.

"I do *wish* we could stay a little longer," Heather said as she hugged Julia. "I hate that we're leaving so soon after what happened."

"Don't worry about us," Barker assured her. "We'll be fine."

"If we could afford to stick around, we would," Casper explained as he hugged Barker with his free arm. "Evelyn is lovely, but her rooms are pricey, free tarot reading or not. Look after yourself, kiddo."

Casper hobbled over to the van and climbed into the passenger seat. Heather went to follow but stopped and snapped her fingers.

"I almost forgot to give you this!" She reached into her handbag, pulled out a small pink envelope, and passed it to Julia. "Your wedding gift. And before you say anything, just accept it. I have no use for it."

"But we didn't get married."

"So, save it for when you do." Heather cupped Julia's cheek and gave it a soft pat. "Stay safe and look after him. He might be forty, but don't let that fool you. He'll always be a baby in my eyes."

With one final wave, Heather climbed into the van, and they set off.

"*My phone!*" Jessie cried as she patted down her jeans. "I think I left it on the table. One second."

Jessie darted back in the restaurant, leaving Julia and Barker on the pavement. Julia looked down at the envelope. It was the only gift they had received; the others no doubt having already been returned. She turned it over in her hands, unsure what to do with it. As though he could sense her reservations, Barker plucked the envelope from her hands and ripped it open.

"*Julia!*" Jessie cried, running out of the restaurant. "You *need* to come and see this!"

Before Julia could ask any questions, Jessie grabbed her and dragged her through the door. She pulled her into the middle of the restaurant and pointed her at lover's corner. Rita and her son were long gone and had been replaced by two people who actually looked like they were on a date.

"Is that *Dot*?" Jessie laughed disbelievingly. "Holding hands with a *man*? What is happening to the world?"

Percy and Dot held hands across the table, a candle flickering between them. Percy pulled one hand away and reached into his inside pocket. Julia and Jessie exchanged startled looks and clung to each other as he pulled out a box. Julia breathed a sigh of relief when she realised that Percy was holding a carton of playing cards.

He shuffled the deck in his hands before offering them to Dot. She plucked one out, looked at it, and put it back. He waved his hand over the deck, shuffled the cards another time, and presented her with a card. Dot tilted her head and shook it. Percy looked disappointed and placed the cards on the table. He split them into two piles and attempted to merge them together like they did in casinos. The cards flew in every direction, causing Dot to laugh in an airy tone Julia had never heard before.

Dot tossed her head back and laughed more as Percy scrambled on the floor to pick up his scattered cards. As she turned to look at him, her eyes drifted to Julia's. Dot immediately looked away. Julia and Jessie jumped out of view, but it was too late; they had been spotted.

"Do we go over?" Jessie whispered. "I'm so confused. That's *Dot*. Dot doesn't date. She's like ... one-hundred-and-twenty-something."

"Let's leave them to it." Julia linked arms with Jessie and pulled her to the exit. "If there's one thing I've learned about my gran over the years, it's to expect the unexpected. There's no predicting that woman."

They walked towards the exit, and even though Julia wanted to be happy for her gran, she couldn't help but remember what Flora had told her about Percy and Gloria. She hoped it would come to nothing, but the knowledge nagged at the back of her mind. Leaving the restaurant, they rejoined Barker on the pavement.

"Dot is in there on a date!" Jessie cried, clapping her hands together. "Brilliant! Absolutely *brilliant*! I need to text Alfie. He's never going to believe what his landlady is up to."

Jessie pulled her phone and keys from her pocket and hurried over to her car. Barker passed Julia the contents of the pink envelope.

"A £10 gift card to *Pet Planet*." Julia turned the wedding present over in her hands. "How ... thoughtful?"

"I sense we've just been re-gifted." Barker turned it over and pointed out the expiry date. "It expires in three days."

Julia tucked the gift card into her bag, grateful all the same. They climbed into the back of the car. Jessie, who was too busy texting on her phone, had yet to notice the yellow parking ticket stuck to the outside of the front window.

9

J ulia couldn't believe a year had passed since her baby brother's birth. It felt like only yesterday that her father and his young wife, Katie, had revealed they were expecting a baby, and even less time since Vinnie's dramatic entrance in the early hours of the morning the day after Barker's ill-fated thirty-ninth birthday party.

To spend the afternoon at Peridale Manor celebrating Vinnie's first birthday with a family tea party was a surreal experience, especially because Julia had spent most of her life exclusively being an older sister to Sue. She had yet to fully wrap her head around having a rambunctious and cheeky one-year-old brother almost four decades her junior.

Despite her initial reservations about her father having an infant at his age, it was impossible not to love Vinnie, especially now that he was growing into his own personality. Watching him wobblily walk around the party gurgling sounds that almost sounded like words melted her heart and made her excited for the day she could sit down and converse with him.

A notable absence from the party was Dot. Julia had a good idea where her gran was, and, more importantly, whom she was with. After leaving the party with a bag of tissue-wrapped cake slices, Julia dropped Jessie and Barker at home and drove into the village. The moment she parked outside Dot's cottage, the heavens opened and rain mirroring that of her wedding day crashed down from the darkened sky. Knowing a gap wasn't likely to come, Julia grabbed the party bag and sprinted for Dot's front door.

Even though Dot rarely gave Julia the courtesy of knocking when she visited, Julia banged on the door as the rain soaked her to her bone. She only waited ten seconds before grabbing the handle. The door opened, but bounced back in its frame, the chain lock stopping her getting any further.

"*Gran?*" Julia cried through the gap. "It's me!"

A stretch of silence followed before Julia heard movement and whispering within the cottage.

"I'm not feeling well, dear!" Dot called back from what sounded like the sitting room. "You get yourself home."

"I'm *soaked!*" Julia began to shiver on the doorstep. "Let me in!"

It took Dot almost a minute to take the chain off the door to let Julia in. Dot appeared flushed from rushing around, and even though she was still in her nightgown, she certainly didn't seem sick.

"You were missed at the party." Julia held up the bag. "I brought you some cake."

"Party?" Dot wrinkled her nose before snapping her fingers. "*Shoot!* Today was Vinnie's party! I'm sorry, dear. When you get to my age, the days all blur into one. I haven't quite wrapped my head around suddenly having a third grandchild."

"I thought you were ill?"

"That too." Dot's cheeks reddened further as she forced a false smile. "Well, thank you for dropping by.

I really must get back."

"Back to what?"

"To being ill?" Dot fiddled with her gown's buttons as her eyes darted to the closed kitchen door at the end of the hall. "What's with all the questions?"

"Aren't you going to invite me in for some warming tea?" Julia motioned to her soaked dress. "I'm freezing."

Dot pursed her lips and squinted down at Julia, and it became instantly apparent that they both knew what was going on. Still, Julia wanted to test her gran and see how far she could push things before she finally started being honest.

"Take a seat in the sitting room." Dot motioned to the door. "I'll make you a cup of your favourite."

Julia nodded and waited for Dot to head to the kitchen, but it was clear she wasn't going to move until Julia was in the sitting room. Julia conceded and walked in, and Dot slammed the door right behind her. Julia listened as her gran hurried to the kitchen, also closing that door behind her.

Perching on the sofa, Julia brushed her wet curls out of her face and scanned the room. At first, nothing looked out of place. A teapot and a plate of leftover toast were on the table, and the TV was on the local news but muted with subtitles. After a second, Julia noticed the second teacup. She stood up and touched them both; still warm.

"Here you go!" Dot announced as she entered the sitting room. "A cup of tea."

Julia wrapped her hands around the cup and let it warm her as she settled into Dot's couch. Dot hovered in the corner before sighing and perching on the arm of the armchair by the fire. Her knee bounced up and down as she stared at Julia's tea. Julia blew on the surface and took a small sip before placing it on the coffee table. Dot sighed audibly.

"Been up to anything fun lately?" Julia asked, clasping her hands together.

"*Fun?*" Dot blushed again, her eyes widening. "Erm, not really, dear. Unless you count drawing my pension? Nothing outside the usual routine. How about yourself?"

"It was Barker's birthday last night. We went out for a quiet meal."

"Oh?" Dot's voice wobbled. "How lovely."

"I saw the most peculiar thing while I was there." Julia leaned on the chair's arm and stared deep into her gran's eyes. "There was a woman who looked *exactly* like you. If I didn't know better, I'd say you had a twin sister."

Dot's fake smile remained for a second, and Julia thought she was going to continue going along with the fun, but she sighed, rolled her eyes, and relaxed.

"I *knew* that was you." Dot pursed her lips. "My long-distance vision has always been exceptional. You've caught me." She stood, walked over to the sitting room door and opened it. "*Percy*! You can come out now."

The kitchen door opened and the short, bespectacled, bald man shuffled out. He smiled uncertainly at Julia as he made his way into the sitting room.

"Good afternoon," he said to Julia. "What terrible weather we're having. Looks like you got caught in it."

"She knows." Dot wafted her hand. "She saw us at the restaurant last night. I told you The Comfy Corner was a bad idea!"

"Actually, I've had my suspicions for a while," Julia revealed. "You've hardly been subtle."

Dot almost looked disappointed that her romance hadn't been as secret as she clearly thought. Percy blushed and pushed his glasses up the bridge of his nose. Dot slid down into the armchair and Percy took the position leaning against the chair's arm. They made such an unlikely couple, and yet their contrasts oddly suited each other. Whereas Dot was tall and slender with her neat and put-together style, Percy was short, with mismatching clothes. He wore black and white chequered trousers held up by red braces, a corduroy waistcoat over a blue shirt, and a pink and yellow bow-tie. His bifocal glasses, which made his pupils twice their natural size, were perfect circles with red frames. He closely resembled a circus clown's clumsy sidekick.

"I just wanted a little fun, dear." Dot shrugged. "You don't get many opportunities at this age to experience these things. Romance is a young person's game. After your grandfather died, I swore I'd never court another man again, but where did that get me? I'm eighty-four! As much as I'd like to pretend that I'm going to live forever, I know I'm not. I could die in my sleep tonight, and where would—"

"You don't have to explain yourself to me," Julia jumped in, holding up her hands. "I'm happy that you're doing something that makes you happy. You didn't need to hide it from me."

"And what about the rest of them?" Dot cast her hand to the window. "The gossips! What would they say? They'd call us foolish! Courting at our age? We should be crawling towards our graves, not reliving our youth."

"But it has been fun, Dorothy!" Percy grabbed her hand and kissed it. "You've made me feel more alive than I have since my Joyce passed. You're a vivacious woman with more life in her than any girl of twenty-two!"

Dot smiled so sweetly at Percy that it melted Julia's heart. Julia hadn't imagined her gran wanting love, and she felt silly for never considering that Dot might like one last great love affair in her twilight years.

"How did you meet?" Julia picked up her tea and sipped from it.

"At the choir. It was my first meeting. Percy came up to me and pulled a bunch of flowers out of his pocket. I thought he was utterly ridiculous, but I liked that. It made me laugh. I invited him over for tea and we realised we had a lot in common."

"Like?"

"Well, singing for one," Dot said, looking up at Percy with adoring eyes. "And he appreciates the old movies and music that I love. There are so few people left from my era who value the old ways. There's nothing wrong with a sprinkle of theatrical spirit every now and then!"

"And we both take a *keen* interest in the

community," Percy added. "We like to know what's going on. Keeping our fingers on the pulse is very important."

"You mean gossiping?"

"I am *not* a gossip!" Dot cried. "I believe in the free flow of information. It's important to know who you're living around! *Unsavoury* characters are hiding in plain sight, ready to jump out and ruin your life at any moment. Your pursuit of all these mysteries has taught us that Peridale is crawling with *insalubrious* folk! It's better we keep the news flowing, so everyone has a fair shot."

"Nicely put, Dorothy." Percy patted her hand. "Couldn't have said it better myself."

It was clear to see they were somehow made for each other. It almost made Julia want to forget that she had added Percy to her list of suspects. For the sake of her gran, however, she couldn't discount the information.

"Have you found anything more about Gloria's murder during your active interest in the community?" Julia asked tactfully.

"Tell her, Percy!" Dot exclaimed, slapping him on the knee. "I've meant to call you all morning, but we got swept up in our conversation."

Percy straightened up and wiggled his bowtie with a pleased smile. Much like Dot, he seemed to feed off 'the free flow of information'.

"After our splendid date at The Comfy Corner— did you try the pigs in blankets pie, Julia?" He waited for her to nod. "Quite delightful, wouldn't you say? Mary and Todd really are geniuses in that kitchen!"

"Stay on track, dear," Dot prompted.

"Right you are!" He nodded. "This is why we work so well. My mind tends to wander, but Dorothy here is as sharp as a knife! Now, where was I?" Percy tapped on his chin before snapping his fingers. "Ah, yes! After our marvellous dinner last night, we retired to The Plough for a late-night tipple. You know how Dot is fond of her sherry, and I don't mind a finger of whiskey of an evening. Truth be told, I was having such a fun time I didn't want to leave this one's side so early."

"Bless you, dear."

"You're most welcome." Percy kissed Dot's hands. "After our beverages, I walked Dot home, and we bid our goodnights. I was going to walk home to my flat on Mulberry Lane when I realised I didn't have my keys with me. I knew I had probably left them at the pub or the restaurant, but it was also a possibility that I had dropped them at the church. I hadn't needed them all day, so I didn't quite remember when I had last had them. With the church being the closest, I started my search there. Letting myself in, I walked up to Father David's vestry. I was about to knock when I realised he was on the phone. Now, it's not in my nature to eavesdrop, but if I happen to hear something I'm not supposed to, that's out of my hands."

Percy paused as he gathered his thoughts. He wiggled his bowtie before hooking his thumbs through his braces.

"Now, I can't be sure of the *exact* context of what I heard, but I know the words I heard." Percy inhaled deeply. "Father David was giving his bank details to someone over the phone. There's nothing out of the ordinary about that, is there? I might be a dinosaur, but even I know it's easier to pay for things over the phone these days."

"Get to the point, dear."

"Right you are." Percy wagged his finger. "Now, after he had finished giving his card details, he said something that made my ears prick up."

"And that was?" Julia prompted.

"His exact words were, 'And are you sure that's it? The £2000 debt is entirely paid off?', and then he said his goodbyes and hung up." Percy clapped his hands together. "That's it! Father David appeared to be paying off a debt over the phone."

"Suspicious, don't you think?" Dot shuffled to the edge of her seat. "A man of God racking up a debt that large? How could he possibly owe that much money to someone?"

"It's not against the law to owe money," Julia said, unsure how to absorb the information. "It could have an innocent explanation."

"It could, but does it?" Dot lowered her voice and looked around. "How well do we *really* know the man? Yes, he's served this village for decades, but what do we know of him outside the church?"

"Being private doesn't mean he's up to no good."

"And I'd usually agree." Percy shook his head. "But, considering everything that has happened with Gloria's death, it seems like odd timing, don't you think?"

"What are you suggesting?"

"Well, I think that Father David somehow profited from Gloria's death." Dot's eyes lit up as she spoke. "He took something of value from her and murdered her to cover his tracks!"

"Father David?" Julia forced a laugh. "This is all very far-fetched!"

"Stranger things have happened," Percy said. "Don't let the robes fool you!"

Julia pursed her lips. Normally, it was bad enough having to contend with Dot's outrageous ideas, but having Percy there only added fuel to the fire. Like the bonfire, they had let their thoughts burn wildly out of control.

Julia was about to turn the conversation back to Gloria, and Flora's claim that Percy and Gloria had once dated, but the front door opened.

"That'll be Alfie," Dot said as he glanced at the clock. "He said he was nipping out to grab some lunch an hour ago."

Julia heard Alfie's deep chuckle, which was quickly followed by a girlish giggle. She wondered if it belonged to Jessie, but she wasn't the type of girl who giggled. Julia looked to Dot for an explanation, but her gran only shrugged. Leaving her tea on the table, Julia stood and crept to the door. Popping her head around the door frame, Julia was surprised to see Alfie and Skye kissing in the hallway, both completely soaked from the rain. Julia cleared her throat.

"*Julia!*" Alfie cried, wiping his mouth after pulling away from Skye. "You got caught in the rain too?"

Skye tucked her wet hair behind her ears as she

smiled awkwardly at Julia. Even with running makeup and her hair plastered to her head, she was beautiful. In the light of Dot's hallway lamp, Julia thought she bore a striking resemblance to Keira Knightley.

"I'll make you that cup of coffee I promised," Alfie said, resting his hand on Skye's arm. "Go and wait in the sitting room."

"I'll make the coffee," Julia offered, sensing her moment to finally get the beauty alone. "Skye, do you mind helping?"

Skye looked at Alfie as though waiting for him to protest Julia's offer, but when he didn't say anything, she turned to Julia and flashed her pretty smile. Julia peeled Skye away from Alfie's side and into the kitchen. She closed the door behind them.

"Terrible weather we're having," Julia remarked, glancing out the kitchen window into Dot's overgrown garden. "Won't be too long before that rain turns to snow."

"I was on my way to Rita's," Skye explained as she mopped her hair with one of Dot's tea towels. "I didn't get very far. I bumped into Alfie on Mulberry Lane, and he invited me back here for coffee."

"You two seem quite smitten with each other."

"I'm not stepping on anyone's toes, am I?" Skye

asked. "Because if I am, I—"

"Not at all!" Julia insisted, giving the young beauty a smile she hoped would relax her. "Alfie is like family to me. I care about his happiness. You seem like a nice girl." She put the kettle on its base and flicked the switch. "You said you were on your way to Rita's? I get the feeling she didn't invite you around. I sat in on the choir meeting the other day. You two didn't exactly seem friendly."

"I wanted to make sure she meant what she said about training my voice to reach its full potential." Skye leaned against the counter and watched as Julia retrieved cups from the cupboard. "If you were at the meeting, you saw what she did to Flora. I needed to know I hadn't let my aunt walk out for nothing."

"Flora's your aunt?"

"Technically." Skye bobbed her head. "My dad is her younger brother, but we've never really been a big happy family. Those two haven't spoken in years. She was rarely there when I was growing up. She was too busy being glued to Gloria's side. I almost walked out when I saw her there on my first day, but she asked me to stay. It's brought us a little closer together, but she's always kept me at arm's length. She has her strange ways about her, don't you think?"

Julia nodded her agreement. She cast her mind back to talking to Flora at the bonfire. When she had asked if Flora had any family, she had only mentioned her estranged brother.

"I think she needs some family right now," Julia said as she scooped coffee into two mugs. "She seems to be going through a tough time coming to terms with Gloria's death."

"I can try, but I don't think I can help her. Now that she's not in the choir, we don't have that space to spend time together. I work every hour I can to pay off my student debts, and when I'm not working, I'm at the choir."

"Were you working the morning of my wedding?" Julia asked. "I didn't see you at the church."

"I was stuck in traffic," Skye said without missing a beat. "A riverbank burst and flooded the roads. I didn't get anywhere near Peridale until way into the night."

Julia poured the boiled water into the mugs. Skye's story slotted right in, but her promptness to establish an alibi felt somewhat forced. Had Alfie mentioned that she was trying to piece together the events surrounding Gloria's death? She considered pushing it further, but she didn't want the young woman to turn on her; she remembered what Dot had said about her being feisty and argumentative.

"Do you have Rita's address?" Julia asked, changing direction. "I want to talk to her about some things."

"Sure." Skye looked around and spotted Dot's shopping list notepad on the wall. She scribbled down an address and passed it to Julia. "It's the giant house at the end of the Longmore Lane. Willow Cottage. You can't miss it."

"Thank you."

"I only know where she lives because she organised a secret meeting a few months ago to put together a rebellion to overthrow Gloria. I was all for it, but the others didn't want to rock the boat, so it didn't go anywhere."

Julia nodded, not wanting to say another word. She passed Skye the two mugs of coffee, wondering if she realised she had not only strengthened Rita's potential motive for murder but her own as well.

Leaving the two freshly-formed couples in the sitting room, Julia slipped out and ran through the rain back to her car. She pulled out the address, but it wasn't a street name she recognised. She punched the address into the GPS on her phone, which revealed Rita lived in Riverswick, Peridale's closet neighbouring village.

She travelled along the narrow, winding lanes out of Peridale, driving carefully in the heavy rain. When she reached the small stone bridge, which had a 'Welcome to Riverswick' sign just ahead of it, she finally saw the extent of the damage caused by the recent rain. The river gushed under the bridge, higher than she had ever seen it. She drove slowly over the bridge, and, in the distance, she spotted a team of workers in high visibility coats trying to fix the burst bank.

"Turn left," the robotic female voice instructed as Julia came off the bridge. "Then continue straight for two hundred yards. Your destination is on the left."

She took the first left turn onto Longmore Lane on the outskirts of the village. As promised, grand homes built of traditional golden Cotswold stone filled the street. Though they were technically cottages, each was triple the size of Julia's modest home. Every home had its own lavish garden, and, even in the rain, Julia could tell they were meticulously looked after.

She reached the end of the lane, where Willow Cottage stood. It was by far the grandest home of them all, suiting Rita's larger-than-life arrogance, but two things set it apart. The first was the unkempt nature of the garden and surrounding hedges, and the second was the 'FOR SALE' sign that jutted out in front of the property.

Already sensing that she had gone on a wild goose chase, Julia left her car and ventured down the weed-covered lawn to the front door. She cupped her hands against the front window, but the cottage didn't have a scrap of furniture inside. She lingered in the rain, wondering where Rita could have gone.

"Can I help you?" a booming voice called from behind her. "You're on private property."

Julia whipped around to see an elderly man in a black raincoat with a beagle at his heels in a matching coat. Knowing she had to come up with something quick, Julia's eyes wandered to the 'FOR SALE' sign.

"I'm supposed to be viewing the property," she called as she ran down the lane. "I think my estate agent hasn't managed to get through the flooded roads."

"We tell the council every year, but do they listen?" The man shook his head. "You'd be better waiting in your car. You look frozen to the bone, you poor thing."

"I just really love this property," Julia lied. "Do you know anything about the people selling it? I can't imagine anyone ever wanting to give this place up."

"It wasn't by choice." The man glanced up and

down the road to make sure they were alone. "I live two doors down, and I saw the *whole* thing. The heavies came from the county court to repossess the place for the bank two months ago. Turfed her out in her pyjamas and only gave her ten minutes to pack her essentials and go. None of us had any idea Rita had fallen so far behind with her mortgage! The way she splashed her cash around, we thought she had a bottomless pit of money, but you don't stay rich by spending it, and that messy divorce didn't help."

"That's terrible."

"Don't feel sorry for her!" the man cried. "She was an *awful* woman. Strutted around like she owned the whole street. Between you and me, we were all glad when she left."

"Where did she go?"

"I heard she moved in with her son." The man looked down at the dog, who was staring at the ground as the rain pounded around them. "I better get this one home. I'm Rodger, by the way. I live with my wife, Mavis, at Apple Cottage two down. We might be neighbours soon! What did you say your name was?"

"I didn't." Julia scrambled for a pseudonym. "I'm Rain. Rain Road."

"Unusual name." Rodger squinted at Julia. "Do

drop by if you end up buying."

With that, Rodger left his new potential neighbour 'Rain Road' alone and took his dog back home. Feeling like the village idiot, Julia hurried back to her car and set off toward Peridale. Instead of going to her cottage, she drove straight to the Fern Moore Estate, where she knew Rita's son, Alec Bishop, lived.

Peridale villagers denied any claim to the troubled housing estate that sheltered hundreds of low-income families, and most avoided the place thanks to its less than favourable reputation. Alec had been the first wedding photographer she had met with, and she had almost thought twice when he gave her his Fern Moore address, but she had adored his work, and his prices were far more reasonable than the competition's.

She pulled up in the courtyard, which was unusually empty thanks to the rain. Without wanting to waste another second getting soaked, she ran around the old playground in the middle of the square and straight for the stairwell that would take her to Alec's flat. She reached the second floor and walked down to Flat 43, retracing her footsteps from memory.

A rumble of thunder echoed behind her as she knocked on the door. To her surprise, the force of her knock sent the door swinging inwards. She stepped back as the door opened fully. Had Alec left the lock on the latch and not realised? She was about to call out, not wanting to intrude, but a pair of black high heels on the floor caught her eye. They jutted out of one of the rooms and pointed straight up. It took Julia a moment to realise they were attached to a pair of feet.

"*Hello?*" Julia called as she crept into the flat. "Is everything okay?"

She heard the fear in her voice; everything was far from okay. A siren blared in the distance as the rain pounded outside, only making the silence within the unlocked flat more evident. She reached the feet and pushed open the door to reveal a photo-developing studio.

Glossy photographs hung from strings above trays of liquid, but they weren't where Julia's attention was drawn. Rita lay stiffly on the floor, swathed in red light. She wore her usual high-necked top and a cream fur coat. Her pearl necklace was missing, but she had a new accessory jutting out of her chest: a large kitchen knife.

10

"They're not linking it to Gloria's death," Barker said after getting off the phone. "Christie doesn't see any pattern."

"Because he doesn't *want* to see a pattern!" Julia cried, slamming her hands on the dining room table. "That man is a stubborn pig!"

"The last thing he wants to do is confirm there might be a serial killer on the loose." Barker rubbed her back. "It would cause a panic."

"But there *is* someone on the loose!" Julia pushed her hands into her curls, already exhausted by the day, even though the sun had only just risen. "He was happy to point out that I was a 'link' between both murders because I 'happened to be there' both times. He drilled me all last night like I was involved! I went to talk to Rita to try and figure out if *she* was the one who killed Gloria, and I ended up the prime suspect."

"Then it's a good thing they confirmed the time of death so quickly." Barker gave her a reassuring squeeze. "She'd been dead for at least twelve hours when you found her, which means we were together in this cottage after my birthday meal."

"And if they hadn't figured that out, they'd be charging me right now." Julia inhaled deeply, wanting to calm herself and not having much luck. "It's so obvious what is happening. Why can't Christie see the connection? Someone is murdering members of the Peridale Harmonics Choir, and I still have no idea why. I should have taken this more seriously from the beginning. I've been going with the flow instead of swimming against the tide."

"You've been through a lot."

"Not as much as Gloria and Rita." Julia sighed and rubbed her temples. "Two women from the same choir are dead. Regardless of how they treated people, they didn't deserve to die. The same person murdered them. I'm *sure* of it."

"I think so too," Barker said softly, "but we need to look at the evidence objectively. Gloria was poisoned, whereas Rita was stabbed. That's not a pattern. It doesn't mean they won't link the two eventually, but they're still gathering evidence for both cases."

"And until then?" Julia shrugged off Barker's hands and stood up. "We wait for more members to die? My gran is part of that choir. What if she's the next target?"

Julia paced the dining room as her mind struggled to filter through the noise. Rita had been her prime suspect, and now she was dead. She dug in her handbag for her notepad and flipped to the page of suspects she had made. Only Skye and Percy were left. Before Julia could think about either, a soft knock sounded at the front door.

"I'll get it," Barker said, brushing his hand over her shoulders as he left the room. "Whoever it is, I'll get rid of them."

Julia stared at the notepad.

Skye.

Percy.

She flipped the page.

Father David.

"Julia?" Barker called. "There's someone here to see you."

She tossed the notepad into her handbag and walked into the hallway, where Alec Bishop stood with a large backpack over his shoulder. He was wrapped up warm, a woolly hat pulled low and covering his blond hair. Red rings circled his swollen eyes, hinting at a sleepless night consumed by tears.

"They said you found her," Alec croaked.

Julia nodded and motioned toward the sitting room. He closed the front door and dropped his bag before following her in. He sat next to Mowgli on the couch, all the life and energy drained from his body. Barker retreated to the dining room, leaving Julia alone with the young man.

"I went to her old cottage in Riverswick," Julia explained after settling into the armchair across from him. "One of the neighbours told me what happened and that she was living with her son. I remembered where you lived from our meeting at the end of summer when I hired you to take pictures for my wedding."

"I should have been there." Alec stared into the fireplace as the wind rattled down the chimney. "I took her out for a meal, and we went back to my flat. Mum wanted to watch a movie, but my friend asked me to go to a bar. Mum told me to go, and I did. I should have gone home after the bar, but I didn't want to wake her. I was drunk. I was five doors down, sleeping on my friend's floor, and she was dead in my flat."

Tears streamed silently down Alec's cheeks. He let them drip into his lap without trying to wipe them away.

"It's not your fault," Julia assured him. "If it hadn't have happened then, it would have happened another time."

"The police said it was a robbery gone wrong." Alec's eyes snapped to Julia's, and he frowned. "All her jewellery was taken. They even took the pearl necklace from around her neck. She had to sell everything from the house, but she refused to let go of her jewellery. One of the last conversations we had was about that stupid jewellery. I took her to The Comfy Corner to try and get through to her. She'd lost everything, and yet she was still spending the little money she had. She'd sell a pair of designer shoes and then spend it on a new handbag. I told her I couldn't look after her forever. I'm going to regret that until the day I die."

Julia wanted to offer words of comfort, but she had no idea what would possibly pull him out of the dark hole his mind had fallen into.

"What was she like as a mother?" Julia asked, wanting to brighten his mood.

"Tough." A half-smile pricked up Alec's lips. "She wanted the best out of everyone and everything. There was no such thing as less than perfect in her world. I didn't really fit into that. She wanted me to go into music, but I never took to it. I'd sit through hours and hours of piano and singing lessons, and she'd hate that I didn't want to try. I was always interested in photography, even as a kid. I'd fill disposable cameras with endless pictures of people and places, and I'd pay to have them developed with my pocket money. I grew up wealthy, but even though she was lavish when it came to buying things for herself, she was frugal when it came to me."

Alec choked on his words and pushed the heels of his hands into his eyes.

"It wasn't even her money," he continued, "it was my father's. She met my dad at the Royal Academy of Music. He came from old money, and she clung to him. He became a composer and earned his own fortune. She tried to get her hands on it in the divorce, but it backfired."

"How so?"

"The lawyers proved she'd been stealing his money for years. She walked away with the bare minimum. It was still a large chunk, but she threw it away. She couldn't seem to understand that money wouldn't keep coming to her like it always had. She treated it like she always had another stash hidden away. I had no idea she wasn't paying for the house until she turned up on my doorstep with her bags. She waltzed in and demanded I let her stay until she found her feet."

Alex paused when Barker slipped into the room with two cups of tea. He placed them on the table and backed out without saying a word.

"That was two months ago." Alec stared at the tea, but he didn't reach out for it. "She never even got close to getting her own place. I don't think she wanted to. She was more bothered about that choir. I kept telling her to find a job, but she acted like the choir *was* her job. She was over the moon when Gloria died because she could finally become the stupid choirmaster. It's all she's talked about for years! They kicked her out of Riverswick's choir because she was always gunning for the top spot. Maybe she thought being in charge would be her ticket to easy street, but I knew it was just another distraction, like the designer clothes and the jewellery."

"She did seem to relish in taking over Gloria's position," Julia said. "That's why I wanted to talk to her. She seemed to know something about Gloria's death. I was at the restaurant when you were. I bumped into your mother in the bathroom. She made a comment about dirty laundry being aired."

"That sounds like my mother." Alec inhaled deeply as he looked up at the ceiling. "She always needed the upper hand. She couldn't bear having people knowing things she didn't. She wasn't the type of woman who could look past her own nose to notice how she affected people. And yet, I'm going to miss her. She was my *mother.* I can't believe she's really gone."

Julia reached out and squeezed his hand. She knew more than anyone what it was like to lose a mother. Alec gave her a thankful smile as he wiped the dampness from his cheeks.

"What will you do now?"

"I'm going to stay with my dad for a while. He's got a new wife and a bunch of awful step-kids, but he lives in a mansion, and there's plenty of space. I can't go back to that flat, and it makes sense to be around family for the time being, especially with Christmas coming up."

"That's wise."

"It's not like my job isn't mobile." He let out a watery half-chuckle before patting down his pockets. "Which reminds me. I wanted to talk to the woman who found my mother, but when I found out it was you, I realised I had to give you this before I left town."

He pulled something small out of his pocket and handed it to Julia.

"What is it?" She turned the small metal oblong around in her hands.

"It's a memory stick. It has the few pictures and videos I got from your wedding. It's all raw and unedited, but I thought they belonged with you. I've meant to bring them around, but there was no urgency until today."

"I don't think I want to see them." Julia held the memory stick out. "I want to forget that day ever happened."

"You don't have to look at them right now," he said as he stood up, "but you might change your mind one day, and if you do, they're there for you. I flipped through a couple of the pictures and despite how things turned out, you really did make a beautiful bride."

Julia stood up and hugged Alec before walking him to the door. He slung his bag over his shoulder and headed out, turning down her offer of a lift to the train station in favour of getting some fresh air. When she closed the door behind him, Barker reappeared in the hallway.

"What did he want?" he asked, his arms folded.

"He just wanted to see the person who found his mother." Julia hid the memory stick in her fist. "For closure, maybe, although I don't think I gave him any. From the way he described Rita, she was hardly going to win any mothering awards."

"Poor guy." Barker sucked the air through his teeth as he glanced at the clock on the wall. "I'm supposed to be having a video call with my publisher at ten. I think they're going to give me the first feedback for the book. I can email and cancel if you want?"

"No." Julia pushed forward a smile. "It's important. You've been waiting for this. I'll be fine."

"It shouldn't take more than an hour. As soon as it's done, we'll crack down on trying to connect the dots between these murders."

"Sounds like a plan."

Barker made a coffee and shut himself in the dining room, leaving Julia to stare at the device in her palm. She hadn't even considered the possibility of hard evidence that she had almost got married, and yet, here it was. She wanted to throw it outside or flush it down the toilet—not that getting rid of it would make a difference. Simply knowing the pictures existed was enough to taunt her.

She held the stick up to her face. She saw two clear options. The first was to put the stick in a drawer and hope she forgot about it until a day she was ready to look. The other was to bite the bullet, swallow the bitter pill, and get it out of the way.

As she made a cup of salted caramel hot chocolate with the recently boiled kettle and some milk from the new fridge that had been delivered yesterday, she concluded there was only one thing to do. She squirted cream and sprinkled marshmallows on top of her concoction, no longer caring that she had a dress to fit into. With her treat, she ventured into the bedroom, closing the door behind her.

She sat in the middle of her perfectly-made bed, the Peridale countryside sprawling out from her bedroom window as the radiator warmed the room. She sandwiched her hot chocolate between her crossed legs and pulled her laptop from her bedside drawer. The screen lit up on the last thing she had been looking at, which happened to be potential honeymoon destinations. They had decided they were going to get away together once Christmas was out of the way to enjoy some winter sun as a married couple. The concept felt so far out of reach, like it belonged to a whole different lifetime.

After a sip of her creamy drink, she plugged the stick into her laptop. A window popped up, covering the holiday website. There were two folders, named 'Pictures' and 'Videos'. She clicked the pictures folder first and watched as over a hundred files loaded in a long list. Unsure where to start, or if they were even in chronological order, she double clicked the one at the top of the list. A picture of the outside of Evelyn's B&B popped up.

Using the arrow keys, she flicked through the pictures. There were more shots of the outside of the B&B, each with different light levels. She assumed these were the test shots to make sure the white balance fitted the weather. When Barker's face popped up, it made her smile. He was in one of the B&B's bedrooms, in a white shirt and underwear as he ironed his jacket. She flicked through again, and he was checking his phone with the iron still on the jacket. The next shot showed smoke rising, and then Alec's hand blurring across the screen. The next had Barker looking at the camera through a crispy hole in his jacket. She couldn't help but chuckle.

While she had been whipping up a new cake and worrying about all the other things that had gone wrong, Barker had endured his own tests. There were pictures of him with Casper and Alfie as they got ready, and then a picture of Evelyn holding up the blue pinstriped jacket he ended up wearing. The next picture was him hugging Evelyn.

Julia was glad she had told the photographer not to come to the cottage. She had wanted a blissful morning living in the moment with her daughter, sister, and best friend. If Alec had been there, he might have captured some lovely shots, but he would have immortalised the chaos forever in images.

Around thirty of the images were of Barker at the B&B before the scenery suddenly switched to the outside of St. Peter's Church. One particular image of the church set against the dark clouds stirred something within her. It looked like a shot from a horror film. After a handful of pictures outside the church, Alec positioned himself in the vestibule and captured the guests as they ran in from the rain. Despite the weather, they all had smiles on their faces; there was no way for them to know what was coming.

She was surprised to see pictures of her and Jessie's cars. She assumed Alec must have ventured into the church when they got out of the car. There were shots of Barker looking nervous, and one of the choir. Dot had yet to arrive at this point, but they were all smiling, except for Gloria, who wore her usual icy scowl, as if she were too serious for such trivial things.

The pictures eventually caught up to what Julia had experienced. There were a dozen pictures of the bridesmaids walking down the aisle. They all looked so beautiful in their cream dresses, and the red roses didn't look nearly as out of place as Julia had feared they would. When she saw the first picture of her dress come up on screen, her heart skipped a definite beat. She froze, her finger unable to skip to the next image. She had the urge to throw the laptop across the room, but she couldn't look away.

"Oh, Julia," she whispered at the picture, "you really did look beautiful."

She skimmed through the pictures and watched as she walked down the aisle with her father. He beamed with pride as he nodded at the guests. Julia was glad she had the veil over her face because she was sure she looked more terrified than was showing.

When she reached the bottom of the aisle, Barker lifted her veil, and the first picture of them facing each other on their wedding morning melted Julia. She almost forgot she was viewing pictures from her life. The couple on screen looked so in love and full of hope as they gazed into each other's eyes. That hope turned to confusion and then horror as Gloria's coughing started. The last two pictures were the hardest to look at.

The penultimate image was a slanted shot of the choir as Gloria struggled to walk away from them. Julia used the magnifying glass tool and zoomed in on each of the choir members' faces. Everyone looked alarmed except for Rita, who seemed to be enjoying her rival's downfall. If she had seen this image when Rita was still alive, it would have cemented her as the prime suspect in Julia's mind.

The final image was blurry, as though Alec was dropping his camera, but Julia could make out Gloria on the floor with Flora by her side. Difficult as it had been to view first-hand, knowing everything that had followed unsettled Julia even further.

She flicked back to the previous image and focused in on Percy's face. He was gasping, eyes wide and mouth agape. If Julia hadn't known the context, she would have thought he was pulling faces in the mirror. Could that face have been responsible for Gloria's death? She wasn't so sure.

The one face she would have paid good money to see was missing from the line-up. Skye, as she had claimed, had been stuck outside of Peridale thanks to the flooding.

Deciding she was finished with reliving the awful day, Julia closed the image preview window. She almost shut the laptop entirely, but she remembered the second folder. She clicked on 'Videos', and only four files popped up. The first was called 'right-angle.mp4', the second 'left-angle.mp4', the third 'bride-groom-closeups.mp4', and the fourth 'time-lapse-shot.mp4'.

Julia was immediately drawn to the fourth clip. One of the things that had convinced Julia to go with Alec was his video producing skill. He had shown her a handful of wedding videos, which had all been shot using high-quality cameras dotted around the church and reception venue. Instead of having a cameraman in the guests' faces, the cameras had been hidden to capture natural reactions, almost like one of the reality television shows Jessie loved watching. One of the things Julia had most enjoyed was the portion of the wedding DVD that had a time lapse of the ceremony, condensing the entire day into a couple of minutes.

She clicked on the file, but to her surprise, the clip wasn't two minutes long, but two hours and thirty minutes long. The camera appeared to be hung somewhere at the front of the church, its frame focused on the doors. She supposed this was to capture all the guests arriving and filling the church. Alec appeared in the middle of the aisle. He gave his thumbs up to the camera before checking something on his phone. When he seemed satisfied, he exited the church, his photography camera around his neck.

The church remained still for nearly a full minute until Father David appeared. He walked into the shot, presumably from his vestry, and he appeared to be reading a letter. He wandered halfway up the aisle before sitting down on one of the pews. He continued to read over the letter, and when he was finished, he pulled off his glasses, wiped them on his robe, sighed, and began to pray. His lips moved in silent prayer as he rocked gently in his seat. She watched him do this for a couple of minutes until she felt uncomfortable. She hovered over the time bar, and a preview of the clip popped up. She dragged it along until something changed.

Fifteen minutes later, Gloria burst through the doors. Father David jumped up and faced the now-deceased choirmaster. He hid the letter behind his back. They talked for a brief moment, but the camera didn't pick up more than a muffled echo. Father David disappeared from the frame, leaving Gloria to walk down the aisle. She also vanished. Julia was about to scrub to the next event, but she heard Gloria singing. She seemed to be practising her solo for the service. Her voice radiated through the laptop's speakers. There was no denying her voice had power.

Julia was so captivated listening to Gloria's off-screen singing, it took her a moment to realise the doors had opened once again.

"You're far too early, Skye," Gloria called. "I'm rehearsing."

"I want to talk to you alone," Skye replied as she marched down the aisle. "I want this solo."

"Tough."

"I mean it, Gloria!" Skye snapped as she walked out of the view of the camera. "You know I'm the better singer."

"I know that, do I?"

"Everyone knows it."

"I don't really care what you *think* you know, little girl. *I* sing the solos. That's how it's *always* been, and that's how it will *stay*."

"Why are you so selfish?" Skye cried. "You know Rita is trying to rally a rebellion against you? She wants your position, and she's promised to be fair with it."

"*Ha!* Rita doesn't have a fair bone in her body. Do you really think the other members will agree to that? *I'm* their leader. You've only been here for five minutes. If you don't like it, you can leave."

"Rita held a meeting." Skye's voice wobbled. "Everyone was there except you and my aunt. They didn't agree to help Rita, but I could feel they wanted change. It wouldn't take much prodding to convince them. If not Rita, then someone else, but everyone is sick and tired of you bossing us around!"

A sharp crack pierced through the speakers, and it was a sound that could only be linked to a hand swiftly striking a cheek. Seconds later, Skye sprinted down the aisle, clutching her face. The doors banged behind her and silence followed.

As though she had witnessed it first-hand, Julia sat in shock and stared at the screen until something else happened. A little while later, Gloria walked down the aisle, leaving the church empty once again.

"Skye lied to me," Julia whispered before sipping more hot chocolate, which was now anything but hot.

There was a bang off-screen, followed by the sound of metal clinking against metal. Julia strained her ears, unsure what she was hearing. The doors at the top of the screen opened again, and Rita marched in, sunglasses over her eyes and a black cardigan billowing around her.

"Oh, it's just you," Rita said as she pulled her glasses off. "Where's everyone else? Don't tell me I got the wrong time. *Wait*, what are you doing?"

There was another second of silence as Rita squinted and walked off-screen.

"Are you stealing all this stuff?" Rita cried, laughter in her voice. "You've got to be kidding me! Are you that desperate for money that you're stealing church trinkets? Give me that bag!"

A noise indicated a small scuffle, and then a crash of metal. A golden chalice rolled onto the bottom of the screen. Rita walked over and picked it up. She held it up to the light.

"Solid gold?" she asked the person off-camera. "I think this tat would sell for a pretty penny." She tossed the chalice off-camera. "Cat got your tongue? I should call the police on you, but I think there's a way this can work for both of us, don't you?"

Rita hurried off-camera. Another soft bang hinted at another door at the back of the church closing. Seconds later, Gloria walked in, this time with a brown paper bag clutched in her hand. Julia watched as she sat in the pews and ate a burger and fries while looking at something on her phone.

Julia scrubbed across the video, bypassing twenty minutes of Gloria sitting in silence on her phone. She resumed watching when the doors opened, and in walked Rita, followed by Shilpa, Evelyn, Percy, Dot, Alfie, and Flora.

"Too good to meet us at the pub?" Rita called, waving a bottle of water in her hand. "Smells like grease in here."

"Give it a rest for once, Rita," Dot said. "You're always harping on about something."

Gloria heaved herself up off the bench and walked over to Rita. Julia thought she was going to slap her like she did to Skye, but instead, she snatched the bottle of water.

"I need this for my voice." Gloria unscrewed the cap and began drinking. She turned around and walked off with a smirk. "Thanks, Rita."

Flora hurried after Gloria, leaving the other members to snicker behind Rita's back. The choir rehearsed off-camera, and a familiar coughing sound echoed around the church. It wasn't as bad as it had been during the ceremony, but it was there. Julia scrubbed along the video. It wasn't long before Dot and

Percy snuck off, and then the guests started to arrive. She closed the video before her appearance; she didn't want to live through it for the third time.

Julia drank the last of her hot chocolate as she mulled over everything the video had revealed. After draining the mug, she swirled the sunken marshmallows and the undissolved gritty mixture in the bottom of the cup.

"The water bottle," Julia said, her eyes widening. "The arsenic was in the water bottle!"

She put the cup on the bedside table and scrambled off the bed. Without giving it a second thought, Julia burst into the dining room.

"Barker, the arsenic was in the water bottle!" Julia cried, her heart pounding a thousand miles a minute. "Remember? Gloria was drinking from a bottle when she started coughing, and it only got worse. A water bottle that Gloria *stole* from Rita to be spiteful. Someone isn't killing off members of the choir, they're just cleaning up their mess. Gloria was never the original target. Rita was!"

11

ater that afternoon, Julia and Barker wrapped
up warm and walked down to the village to
peruse the Christmas market that travelled
across the Cotswolds during the festive period,
spending a week in each location. This year, Peridale
was hosting the grand opening of the market, and it
appeared most of the village had flocked to the green
to see what was on offer. Now that Halloween and

Bonfire Night had passed, gears had naturally shifted, and the Christmas spirit was well and truly in the air.

"Explain it to me again," Barker said as they walked down the first row of wooden cabin stalls. "I need to get my head around this before we take it to DI Christie."

Julia inhaled, the scent of mulled wine from one of the stalls making her wish things were normal so she could enjoy the market. She looked towards her café, down at the end of the row. It saddened her to know she wasn't part of the event this year, and even though she would love to reopen, she knew it was wise to wait until Monday as originally planned.

"Rita caught someone in the act of stealing valuables from the church," Julia explained again, taking her time to slow down. "She alluded to the person needing money, and then insinuated that they could both benefit from the theft."

"So, whoever she caught red-handed is the person who poisoned Gloria?" Barker scratched at his head through his hat. "But they never meant to poison Gloria, they really wanted to poison Rita?"

"If my theory is correct, whoever dropped that arsenic into Rita's water did it at The Plough." They paused at a stall selling carved Christmas tree decorations. "I thought the poisoner was either trying to send a message or just in a rush. What if it was both? They wanted to show Rita they couldn't be blackmailed, and they didn't have long to do it."

"She could have given them an ultimatum?" Barker suggested as he picked up a carved angel. "But don't you think that seems drastic? Killing Rita over some stolen church stuff? If they'd just put the things back, they would have got a slap on the wrist. Why resort to murder?"

"Desperation? Maybe they weren't thinking straight. It all happened so fast, after all. They'd had to have left the church, sourced the arsenic, and then slipped it into Rita's bottle at the pub without her noticing."

"I bet they were watching her the whole time, waiting for her to take a sip." Barker put the angel back, and they continued down the row. "And it has to be someone who knew they were meeting at the pub, which keeps it confined to those who sang at the wedding."

"Not necessarily," Julia mused, looking around to make sure they weren't being listened in on. "Remember what I told you about Skye's lie? She told me she didn't get to Peridale until later that evening,

179

but I have video proof that she was here in the morning. She confronted Gloria and then vanished. Nothing says she didn't come back to rob the place, get the arsenic, and go to the pub anyway."

"But then where did she go?"

"Would you stick around if you'd slipped arsenic into someone's drink?"

"Good point." Barker nodded. "So, why come back to the choir? Why not run away?"

"That would make it obvious. And she loves singing. She wanted that solo. I doubt she cared that she killed Gloria by accident. She waited things out before paying Rita a visit to finish the job."

"It all makes sense," Barker said as they turned the corner and set off up the next row of stalls. "But, realistically, it could have been any of them. If we bring all this to Christie, he's going to pull each of them in and see whose alibi doesn't line up for both murders."

"That's if he believes us." Julia reached into the pocket of her coat and pulled out the memory stick. "Even with this footage, it's still only a theory."

"A better theory than any he's working with, I suspect."

"I forgot to ask how your video meeting went. Did they like the book?"

"Oh, it went..." Barker's voice trailed off as they turned onto the next row of stalls. "You've got to be kidding me!"

Julia followed his eye line to the end of the row, where the remaining members of the choir were setting up a small stage area.

"They don't wait around, do they?" Julia muttered under her breath. "Two choirmasters dead in less than a week, and yet the show still goes on."

A small crowd gathered in front of the stage, no doubt eager to see what the choir were going to do in the wake of the recent tragedies. Julia and Barker lingered at the back and watched as the choir finished getting ready. Dot spotted them and waved before she pressed a button on a portable CD player. A crackly backing track for 'O Holy Night' played through the small speakers, catching the attention of the idle shoppers who had yet to notice what was happening. Julia wasn't surprised when Skye stepped forward to take the lead vocals, but she was surprised, and pleased, to see that Flora had been reinstated in the choir.

From the moment the first note left Skye's mouth, Julia knew she was something special. Up until now, she had only heard people talk second-hand about Skye's raw talent, but to hear it with her own ears gave her tingles. Her voice was airy, and yet it had enough power to captivate everyone's attention. It was nothing short of angelic.

When the song ended, everyone applauded, including Julia. She almost forgot she was cheering for her new prime suspect. The choir continued onto 'The First Noel', followed by 'Away in a Manger'. They finished their set with a rousing rendition of 'Joy to the World'. The crowd erupted as the choir took their final bow, and, from the smiles on the faces of the choristers, it was clear they had enjoyed every second of their time in the spotlight.

The choir exited the stage, making way for a solo guitarist who looked more than a little disappointed when the crowd dispersed. Sensing her chance to grab Skye, Julia pushed through the moving shoppers, leaving Barker behind. The choir stood behind the stage, all smiles as they talked about their performance. Skye and Alfie were holding hands.

"That was incredible," Julia congratulated them. "Skye, your voice is something else. I had no idea. You're a real star."

"Thank you." Skye fanned her blushing face. "I've never felt anything like it! That was exhilarating. I could have stayed up there for an hour."

"You did great," Alfie said with a cheery smile. "You *finally* had your time to shine."

Julia waited until the choir naturally broke apart, and when Alfie and Skye set off into the market, she followed right behind them.

"*Wait up!*" she called when they reached a German bratwurst stall. "I wanted to talk to you both about what happened to Rita."

"I couldn't believe it when I heard," Alfie said. "She wasn't the nicest woman, but to be stabbed to death for her jewellery? It doesn't seem fair."

"And after what happened to Gloria," Skye added, her brows tilting down. "I almost didn't want to sing today because of it, but we were already booked to perform. It was the first and only thing Rita did for our choir, but it's a step in the right direction."

Julia trained her eyes on Skye as she spoke, but she was either telling the truth, or she was as good an actress as she was a singer.

"I think the murders are connected," Julia admitted, not wanting to beat around the bush. "I think the original poisoning was intended for Rita, and Gloria was caught in the crossfire."

"Why would someone want to poison Rita?" Alfie asked, his brow creasing.

"It's a long story." Julia didn't want to give everything away in front of Skye. "Where were you both on Tuesday night? That's when Rita was stabbed in her son's flat. I'm going to the police with some new information later today, and it's going to put you all in the spotlight."

Skye and Alfie glanced at each other, and it seemed neither could believe Julia was asking for their alibis. Julia tried to assure Alfie with her eyes that she wasn't asking him.

"We were at the cinema," Skye said. "We went to see that new horror film. Didn't we, Alfie?"

"Yeah," he replied quickly. "We were at the cinema."

"We were together all night," Skye added, linking her arm through his.

Julia narrowed her eyes on Alfie. He smiled back at her, but his expression was uneasy. He lifted his hand and rubbed his tattoo-covered neck, his gaze drifting away from Julia's. She wondered if they had gone to the same film Billy and Jessie had seen on Bonfire Night, the night before Rita was killed. If so, she was certain Jessie had said they were watching the final showing.

Before she could push them further, Barker appeared in the crowd and ran towards her, his face twisted.

"Something's happening at the church," he said, panting as he caught his breath. "You need to come and see this."

Barker wrapped his hand around Julia's, and they ran to the top of the row. A crowd had gathered outside the church, but Julia could still see two police cars parked outside.

"They're searching the place again," Barker said. "Christie must be onto something."

They watched on in silence as the crowd around them aired their speculations.

"Do you think there's been another murder?"

"*Another* one?"

"Could be!"

"This village is *cursed!*"

"It *would* be on Christmas market day! I've been looking forward to this *all* year."

The church doors opened, and DI Christie walked out, his eyes averted. He held the doors open for two uniformed officers who were stood on either side of Father David. When people realised the vicar's hands were cuffed behind his back, a gasp rippled through the crowd. Julia's hand drifted up to her mouth. The vicar was led solemnly and quietly to one of the cars. He didn't say a word, nor did he look up. He bowed into the car with silent dignity while the pin-silent crowd watched on.

"I'm going to find out what's going on," Barker said before pushing through the crowd towards the church.

Julia hung back, not wanting to step on DI Christie's toes, especially after their interview at the station. There was no guarantee Christie would tell Barker anything, but the two were former colleagues and friends, and Christie still owed Barker a backlog of favours.

"*Julia!*" Dot cried as she weaved through the crowd. "There you are! What's going on?"

"They've arrested Father David."

"*He* did it?" Dot gasped. "I *told* you he was up to something! I bet this has something to do with that phone call Percy overheard! You can't trust anyone these days."

Julia nodded at her gran, mainly because she wasn't in the mood to argue. No one could say anything to convince her of Father David's guilt. She had put him on her list of suspects, but only because she'd had so little to go on. Seeing him in the frame for real rid her mind of any doubt. There were few people she would have sworn were decent and good human beings to the core, but Father David was one of them, and he had proven that to the village time and time again. She should have been surprised at how quickly people in the crowd were turning against him, but she wasn't. They were hungry for the next scrap of gossip, and they would stop at nothing until they had drained the victim's blood and picked their bones clean.

Barker pushed back through the crowd. He grabbed Julia and pulled her away to the edge of the green, away from prying ears.

"It's not looking good." Barker's eyes darkened. "Christie is convinced he's found his guy. An anonymous letter showed up on the desk at the station. Nobody knows how it got there, but it told them to look in Father David's desk to solve the mystery."

The police car containing Father David drove past. Julia tried to catch his eye through the window to offer some reassurance, but he didn't look up.

"What did they find?"

"The stolen items." Barker gulped. "Father David reported them as missing on the day of Gloria's death."

"Why would *he* report them if *he* took them?" Julia could hear the exasperation in her voice. "Christie sees what he wants to see because he's desperate to wrap this up in a neat bow before Christmas."

"There's more." Barker sighed, his head dropping. "They found the arsenic with the items. As far as Christie is concerned, the case is as good as solved."

Julia could hardly believe what she was hearing. The urge to run to the station to blast Christie took over her. Not a cell in her body believed Father David would murder members of his own church's choir.

"This is too convenient. A letter shows up telling them exactly where to look to find crucial items and they just *believe* it?"

"Wouldn't you?"

"I'd question *how* the anonymous letter writer knew the *exact* location of the items." Julia cast an eye to the church; the gathered crowd had yet to move. "Unless, of course, the sender of the letter *put* the items there to frame Father David."

"Why would someone do that?"

"Because Father David owed a lot of money to someone." Julia tapped her finger against her chin. "The police are going to rip his recent activity to shreds. They're going to find out about his debts, giving them evidence and a motive. If he doesn't have a solid alibi, the case is built for them."

"And now they have a suspect in custody, they're going to be less wary about throwing Rita's murder into the mix." Barker pinched between his eyes. "I know how this game works. They think they have all the jigsaw pieces in front of them, so they're going to slot them together, regardless of the fit."

"These are puzzles from two different boxes," Julia said as a gust of icy wind whipped at her curls. "These murders were driven by money and the lack thereof. Gloria and Rita were killed because the murderer was desperate for cash. They took Rita's jewellery, even going as far as ripping her necklace off her dead body. Few people would do something like that, and I'm certain Father David isn't one of them."

"*Our rings!*" Barker exclaimed, clicking his fingers together. "We still haven't found our wedding rings! What if that same person took those too?"

Julia's mouth curved into a hard smile as she considered the connection.

"If that's true, it had to be someone who was in the church while we waited for the ambulance to arrive." Julia cast her mind back to that long, awful hour. "Most of the guests had already gone, leaving our families, Father David, and the choir members. I definitely don't remember seeing Skye there. She could have slipped in when I wasn't paying attention, but she claims she was with Alfie the night Rita was stabbed."

"And we can rule out our families," Barker added. "And if the same person stole the rings, I'm even less inclined to believe Father David is part of this. Trinkets and jewellery are one thing, but wedding rings? I don't believe a vicar would stoop that low, debt or not." Barker paused, his brow creasing. "Wait, how do you even know Father David owed money?"

Julia had a lightbulb moment as her own jigsaw pieces slotted into place.

"Because Percy told me so!" she cried. "He told me he overheard the vicar paying a £2000 debt over the phone. Percy didn't mention that anyone else was there, so it's possible he's only told Dot and me so far."

"Which means the person who wrote the letter had to have known about Father David's debt to make the frame job even remotely plausible!"

Julia's mind ran through a dozen dizzying thoughts as she spun around and searched the crowd of shoppers for Percy's eccentric clothes. At his height, he could have been anywhere, so she switched to looking for Dot, but her gran was also nowhere to be seen, despite having been there less than ten minutes ago.

"We need to talk to him," Julia said desperately. "Time is running out. Let's split up and look for him. If we don't find him, let's at least find out where he lives.

He said something about living in a flat on Mulberry Lane."

"Someone will know which flat it is."

A lump rose in Julia's thought as she fought back panic.

"We need to be quick," she ordered. "My gran is too close to him. She might not be safe."

12

Julia and Barker spent the better part of fifteen minutes searching the Christmas market for Percy, but he wasn't there. They met where they had started, each with the same tip-off regarding Percy's address. Without wasting a moment, they walked through the busy village to Mulberry Lane, which was crawling with shoppers who had spilt over from the market.

"Shilpa said he lived in the flat above the men's clothes shop," Julia said as they looked down the packed street. "Can you see it?"

"The one I buy my clothes from is at the end of the street." Barker nodded down the road. "But look there. A new one has opened up where the bridal boutique used to be."

"Then we split up and—"

"Look for clues?" Barker chuckled. "I'll take the old bridal boutique."

Leaving Barker behind, Julia weaved in and out of the shoppers, slowly making her way down the narrow pavement. With the twinkling Christmas lights strung between the two sides of the street and the beautiful Christmas displays in the shop windows, it was easy to forget they were still in November. If her gran were there with her, she would have made a comment about how Christmas was starting earlier every year.

Julia reached the bottom of the street. Her father's antique barn seemed to be busier than ever with the festive shoppers out in full force. She turned to Gentlemen's Club, the shop Barker bought his clothes from. It teemed with people despite it having the least festive display on the street. Three mannequins stood proudly in the window, each wearing a fitted suit. The only nod to the holidays was a spattering of sprayed on fake snow in the corners of the window.

The door to the flat above was recessed into the old stone. She walked up the two short steps and looked at the intercom system on the wall, but it provided no hint at who lived above. She pressed the buzzer and waited for a response.

"No luck at mine," Barker said when he rejoined her. "Although, the nice lady called Audrey who lives there called me 'handsome' and invited me in for soup."

"How could you decline such a kind offer?" Julia pressed the buzzer again. "I don't think anyone's home."

"I could check with the shop owner?" Barker offered. "I'm on quite good terms with Jimmy after I signed a stack of my books for him. He thinks they're going to pay to send his kids to university one day."

Barker ventured into the shop, leaving her to step out onto the pavement. She looked up at the flat above the shop. A grin spread across her face when she saw a pair of familiar circular red glasses poking through the curtains. Percy saw her and darted back. Knowing there was nowhere to hide, Julia pressed the buzzer again.

"H-hello?" Percy's voice crackled over the speaker. "Who is it?"

"It's Julia," she called. "Dot's granddaughter. I need to talk to you."

"Now's not a good time, dear."

"It's urgent."

There was a long pause, and Julia imagined the man panicking upstairs. As far as Julia knew, the flat had only one exit, and she was standing in front of it. Just when she thought she might have to wait all night, the intercom buzzed, unlocking the door.

Leaving Barker in the shop, Julia ventured inside. She walked up a plainly decorated staircase to Percy's door, which was open for her arrival. She stepped inside, surprised by how darkly decorated the flat was. The walls were burgundy, hung with framed posters of famous magicians. There was no television, just an old-style radio in the middle of a dark chestnut coffee table. Elvis crooned gently, asking "Are you lonesome tonight?"

Percy appeared from the kitchen with a tray containing a teapot, two cups, and a plate of chocolate digestive biscuits. The kitchenware rattled as he set it down on the coffee table.

"Dot said you like a strange type of tea, but I'm afraid I only have black." Percy motioned for Julia to sit on his dark floral sofa. "To what do I owe the pleasure of your company this afternoon? I was just relaxing after our performance at the market. I'm not really one for shopping, and there is such a thing as too much excitement when you get to my age."

Julia sat down and watched as he poured her a cup of tea. He offered her milk and sugar, but she declined. Remembering how Gloria had died, she decided she wasn't going to bring the cup to her lips.

"I assume you heard about Father David's arrest?" Julia asked as she rested the cup on her knee.

"I did!" Percy poured himself a cup of tea and added plenty of milk. "I saw the commotion at the church, but I couldn't quite see over the crowd. I was rather shocked when Dorothy told me what was going on."

"You were?"

"Of course!" Percy slurped his tea as he settled into the armchair across from Julia. "I know I overheard his telephone conversation, but I didn't really think he was involved. Who would expect a man of God to resort to murder?"

Julia narrowed her eyes. She wanted to figure the man out, but she couldn't see if anything more lay beneath his sweet exterior.

"I heard you were once an item with Gloria." Julia prompted, changing direction. "That's what Flora said, at least."

"I wouldn't exactly say we were 'an item', dear." Percy chuckled as he placed his cup on a side table. He fiddled with his bowtie. "Do you like magic?"

"Magic?"

"*Tricks!*" Percy pulled a pack of cards from his pocket. "I was quite the magician back in my day." He shuffled the cards before holding them out to Julia. "Pick a card but don't show me."

Julia plucked a card from the pack. Four of diamonds. When instructed, she placed it back in the deck and watched Percy reshuffle them. He waved his hand over the deck and pulled up the top card.

"Was *this* your card?"

Julia shook her head at the three of spades.

"Oh, *rats!*" he cried as he slotted the cards back in the breast pocket of his shirt. "I fear I've lost my touch with age. The Magic Circle would revoke my membership in a heartbeat if they knew. Still, I was quite good back in my day." He nodded at a poster on the wall. "They called me *Percival the Great*. Oh, it was a lot of fun. I travelled all over the Cotswolds with my act. Those days are far behind me now."

The poster depicted a cartoon rendering of Percy in a top hat and cape. He wore his round glasses, but he appeared much younger and had a full head of hair.

"I retired decades ago," he explained. "But I never lost the bug! Nothing brings me more joy than tricking someone with a sprinkle of magic, but it's a young man's game. Where was I?"

"Gloria."

"Ah, right you are!" He wagged his finger as he readjusted himself in his seat. "I enjoyed a decade of retirement, but I was itching to get back on the stage if only one more time. The spotlight is a tempting mistress. I never knew how much I craved the audience's energy until it went away. I'm eighty now, but I wanted to do one last show before I turned seventy, so I must have been sixty-nine at the time. I announced one final show to end all shows. *The Return of Percival the Great!* I expected it to be a little show at the village hall with a dozen or so people, but tickets sold out."

Percy paused and sipped his tea.

"It stroked my ego a little too much, pushing me to announce a week of shows," he continued. "They all sold out too! It was going to be my big send-off. One last bite of the apple before I finally settled down into my old age." He paused to sip his tea as he stared at the poster on the wall. "Of course, it was an epic failure! Most of my tricks went wrong on the first night. I picked Gloria at random from the audience to be the woman I sawed in half. The box couldn't sustain her weight, so the bottom caved, ruining the whole illusion! I was laughed off stage. Word got around, and by the end of the week, most people had asked for refunds."

Percy shook his head and exhaled.

"Gloria came back for the final show, and we somehow ended up having a drink together at The Plough. She was twenty years younger than me, so I knew it was never going to work, but it was fun to have some female attention. My poor Joyce was taken from me before I retired, so I'd been rather lonely in this little flat on my own."

"What happened with you and Gloria?"

"We went on a couple of dates, but it was obvious things weren't going to work. I called things off before they got too serious."

"Flora said Gloria ended things."

"Well, she would say that!" Percy laughed. "She was one of the reasons things weren't going to work. She kept turning up on every date and inserting herself into it. Gloria didn't seem to mind, but I did! And then Gloria expected me to pay for everything. I know it's the gentlemanly thing to do, but I was, and still am, a pensioner! My years on the stage didn't bring me riches. After forking out all those refunds, I was scraping by, and paying for Gloria's three-course meals wasn't in my budget. Oh, that woman could eat! Still, things ended amicably, and I joined the choir soon after. It gave me something to do with my days, and I got to enjoy a bit of performing again, even if Gloria always insisted on being the centre of attention."

"And what about Rita? What was your relationship like with her?"

"I didn't have one, dear." Percy frowned before sipping his tea. "I don't want to speak ill of the dead, but I don't think I ever said two words to the woman. Rita was only ever concerned with Rita. I doubt she even knew I was there half the time." Percy paused and looked down into his tea. His expression softened, and he looked up at Julia with a sad smile. "You think it was me, don't you?"

"I-I-I—"

"Your grandmother told me all about your gift for unravelling a mystery." Percy pulled a silk cloth from his pocket and wiped his glasses. "I can assure you, dear, I had nothing to do with their deaths. Why would you think I had?"

"Because you knew about Father David's debt," she explained. "Someone wrote to the police to tell them to search the church. They arrested Father David because they found the stolen church items and the arsenic in his vestry."

"What stolen church items?" Percy put his glasses back on. "I can assure you, this is the first I'm hearing about it."

Julia instantly wanted to believe him, but a voice in the back of her head reminded her not to trust him. He had, after all, admitted that he loved playing tricks on people. Had his years on the stage perfected his acting skills?

"Rita caught someone stealing from the church on the morning of my wedding." Julia leaned forward and placed the untouched cup on the table next to the radio exclusively playing Elvis tunes. "Rita was the target all along. Gloria stole Rita's water bottle, which I suspect had the arsenic in it."

"Yes, the water bottle." Percy nodded. "I was there when she took it. Gloria was always doing things like that to people. She had a nasty edge to her that always came out in those choir meetings. I saw a softer side to her on our handful of dates, but I don't think many got to see that. Why on earth do you think *I* would want to kill either of those women?"

"For the money."

"*Money?*" Percy chuckled as he bobbed his head from side to side. "What do I want money for? Look around you, dear. I have a roof over my head, clothes on my back, food in the cupboards, and, now, the company of a great woman. Money is temporary. It comes and goes, and you can't take it with you. I only have a few years left on this planet, if I'm lucky. I'm fortunate to still have my mind and health. Why would I want to jeopardise being a free man in the last act of my life for something as pointless as money, especially when I have found the one thing I thought I would never experience again."

"But you were the only one who knew about Father David's debt," Julia said, hearing the desperation in her tone. "Unless you told people?"

"I told Dorothy and you, but that's it." Percy paused to think. "If I overheard that phone conversation, it's more than likely that others overheard other phone calls, and that's only if Father David really is innocent. Have you considered that he might be guilty?"

Julia shook her head. She wanted the comfortable couch to swallow her up and take her away from Percy's flat. She had been in such a rush to question him, she hadn't taken a second to consider the likelihood that she might be jumping the gun.

"So, where were you on the night Rita was murdered?" Julia asked. "You said you lost your keys and that's when you went to the church and overheard Father David on the phone. Rita was killed around that time, so where did you go after the church?"

Percy opened his mouth, but whatever he might have said was cut off by a high-pitched sneeze coming from a door next to the kitchen. Julia turned to the door as another louder sneeze followed the first. Without waiting for an explanation, Julia jumped up and walked over to the door. She turned back and looked at Percy before opening it.

"*Gran*?" Julia cried as she stared down at Dot, who was crammed on the floor between a mop bucket and a vacuum cleaner. "What are you doing down there?"

"Hiding from you." Dot held a hand out. "Help me up, dear."

Julia pulled Dot up off the floor. She stepped out of the cupboard as she dusted down her navy pleated skirt. She shook out her short grey curls and adjusted her brooch.

"I thought you were here to give Percy 'the talk'," Dot said as just closed the door behind her. "The 'hurt my grandmother, and I'll chop off your fingers' talk.

We panicked, so I hid. I wanted to eavesdrop, but you were speaking far too quietly."

"She thinks I killed Gloria and Rita," Percy announced from his seat as he sipped his tea. "Thinks I needed the money."

"She did?" Dot waved her hand with a chuckle. "Oh, Julia! I think you're losing your touch. Why would Percy want to kill those silly women?"

"That's what I said," Percy added. "She wants to know where I was on the night Rita was murdered. Should you tell her, or should I?"

Julia and Dot walked back to the couch. They sat across from Percy, and Dot reached out and plucked a biscuit from the plate. She offered one to Julia, who took it because she felt ridiculous for thinking they'd been poisoned.

"After our date at The Comfy Corner and our tipple at the pub, he walked me home and left," Dot mumbled through a mouthful of digestive. "He came back ten minutes later telling me he'd lost his keys. I invited him in for a nightcap, and, well, he ended up staying the night."

"Oh." Julia choked on her biscuit.

"Not like *that*, dear," Dot said, pursing her lips. "We're not like you young whipper-snappers doing all that nonsense before marriage! I poured us a drink, and I borrowed Alfie's computer-tablet thingy. What it's called again, dear?"

"*U*-pad?" Percy said. "Or a *me*-pad? Something like that."

"*iPad*," Julia corrected him.

"That's it!" Dot slapped her leg. "Marvellous invention! I wish we'd had those back in my day. I don't think I would have left the house. No wonder kids today are so fat!" Dot took another bite of her biscuit. "Alfie showed me how to watch films. You click a button, and there they all are! Hundreds of them! It's like someone put the silver screen into a computer. We fell into a hole of watching movie after movie. It's hard not to when all you have to do is click."

"The kids call it 'binge-eating'," Percy said with a knowing nod.

"Binge-*watching*," Julia corrected again.

"We watched *All About Eve, Ben-Hur, Singin' in the Rain, Some Like it Hot*, and *The Bridge on the River Kwai*," Dot continued. "All the classics."

"They don't make them like that anymore." Percy stabbed his finger on the chair arm. "It's all crash, bang, and wallop now! Nobody tells *real* stories."

"We didn't realise what time it was until the birds

started chirping," Dot said. "Percy still didn't have his keys, and I didn't want him wandering around the village looking for them all night, so he slept on my couch. When you caught us out after I missed Vinnie's party, we'd only just woken. I felt like a teenager again! It'd been many decades since I'd stayed up to see a sunrise."

"Apart from ten minutes when I was at the church," Percy said, turning to Julia and smiling, "I was with Dorothy all night. Unless you think I could have run to Fern Moore and back in that time, I think you'll agree that I couldn't possibly have murdered Rita."

"Easy mistake, dear." Dot patted Julia on the shoulder. "You can't get it right every time. Back to the drawing board!"

Julia was too embarrassed to say another word. She finished her biscuit and left them to enjoy the rest of their afternoon together.

Mulberry Lane was even busier, with more of marketgoers making their way to the historical shopping street. Julia looked around for Barker, whom she spotted helping her father at the antique barn. As she crossed the road to tell him what she had found out, her phone rang in her handbag. She pulled it out, surprised to see that Alfie was calling her.

"Julia? It's me. I need to see you."

"What's wrong?" Julia replied as she waved to Barker who had spotted her.

"I'm at my builder's yard," he replied. "Can you come now? I need to speak to you face to face."

Julia hung up and walked to the builder's yard, which was situated at the bottom of a narrow lane behind the antique barn. The chatter of the crowd died away, replaced by the grinding of an electronic saw. When she reached A to B Builders Yard, which was run by Alfie and Billy, she saw Billy cutting through lengths of wood with a giant circular saw. Jessie sat on a barrel behind him, her face buried in her phone. Neither noticed her as she walked towards Alfie's office, which was up a flight of rickety wooden stairs in the main building.

Alfie jumped up from behind his desk when Julia opened the door. He had changed into his filthy blue overalls, which were rolled up at the sleeves to show his completely inked skin. Alfie had been in their life since April and had integrated well into Peridale. A building job had brought him to the village, but finding Jessie, the long-lost sister who had been ripped away from him and put into the care system when she was a baby, was what had kept him here.

"That was quick," Alfie exclaimed as he pulled out a seat for her.

"I was only on Mulberry Lane." Julia sat in the seat and watched as Alfie closed the blinds that looked out onto the courtyard. "You sounded distressed on the phone."

"That's one word for it." Alfie paced in front of the closed window, his fingers in knots. "I wanted to tell you right away, but I felt like I was put on the spot. I called the second I was alone."

"Tell me what?"

"I lied to you." Alfie's pacing came to a halt. "Well, I went along with a lie, which is as good as lying. It took me by surprise, and I didn't know how to come clean in the moment."

Julia had an idea what he was talking about, but she wanted to hear it from his lips. She nodded for him to continue. He sat down, and his tattooed fingers drummed on the surface of his desk.

"I wasn't at the cinema with Skye on the night Rita was killed," he started, the drumming intensifying. "I was at Malcolm Johnson's house until the early hours, fixing his roof in that awful rain. I didn't see Skye at all that day."

"I suspected as much."

"You *did*?" Alfie's fingers stopped drumming. "Why didn't you say anything?"

"I didn't want to reveal my hand to her." Julia leaned back in her chair and rubbed at her forehead; the whiplash of the day was giving her a headache. "She wasn't very convincing, and I was sure the film she said you saw had its last viewing the day before."

"She just blurted it out, and I felt like I had to go along. I didn't want to embarrass her."

"Did she explain why she lied?"

"She doesn't trust you."

"I wonder why." Julia chuckled. "Things are hardly looking good for her, are they? This is the second time I've caught her lying about her alibi. She said she wasn't in Peridale on the morning of my wedding, but I have video proof to show she was."

"Do you think she's behind all of this?"

"I don't know," Julia admitted. "But the fingers are starting to point in her direction."

"I really like her," Alfie said, his voice low. "Have I been a fool?"

"Not a fool, no." Julia offered him a smile. "You're just seeing the best in her. It happens to all of us. I know I've been guilty of that on more than one occasion. Don't beat yourself up over it."

"There's more." He exhaled. "I lent her some money."

"How much?"

"£500."

"Oh, Alfie…"

"I *know!*" he cried. "I *am* a fool. She's in debt up to her eyeballs from her student days. She took out loans all over the place to get through. She kept talking about all the letters she was getting from people saying they were going to her house to take her stuff. I felt bad for her, so I asked how much it would take to at least pay off one letter. I make a decent living here, and I don't like to see people suffer like that. She was in tears."

"Do you know where she is?" Julia asked as she stood up. "I really need to talk to her."

Alfie joined Julia in standing. "She left almost immediately after you spoke to us at the market. I've tried calling her since, but she's not picking up."

"Where does she live?"

"I don't know." Alfie shrugged. "We've only really been seeing each other in the village. I think she mentioned something about living in Riverswick, and I know she works at the cinema in Cheltenham."

"Call me if you see or hear from her." Julia walked towards the door before turning back to Alfie. "Thanks for being honest with me."

Leaving Alfie to get on with his work, Julia snuck out of the builder's yard and hurried back to Mulberry Lane. Barker was still at the antique barn, helping Julia's father lift a mahogany dresser into the back of a white van. She hung back and waited for him to finish. The second he did, she pulled him away from the action.

"It's Skye," Julia said. "I think she's behind all this."

13

J ulia and Barker immediately handed their information to DI Christie, including the video footage showing Skye in the village when she claimed to have been stuck in the floods. Julia had only done so because she hoped Christie would put his ego aside to assess their findings with an open mind; she should have known better.

Despite her theory, Christie only saw what he wanted to see, which was Father David reading a letter in the pews and then someone stealing the items and being caught by Rita.

"It could be *anyone!*" he had said. "This proves *nothing!*"

The only thing he did listen to was Julia's insistence that the two crimes were linked. When she pointed out that Gloria stole a water bottle from Rita and almost immediately began coughing, Christie's ears pricked up, no doubt pleased he could 'solve' two cases with one vicar-shaped stone.

He also didn't care about Skye's numerous lies about her whereabouts, saying 'anyone' would have lied if someone with Julia's 'reputation' started 'ramming them with questions.'

They left the station full of frustration. Later that night, Christie called to say they were charging Father David and had denied him bail until his court hearing.

People in the village seemed happy to accept Father David's guilt, but the thought of the vicar sitting in a lonely cell while he waited for his fate to be decided by other people only lit a fire under her backside.

She spent all the next day searching for Skye. She asked each member of the choir if they knew where she lived; none did. She drove out to the cinema Skye worked at only to find she hadn't turned up for her shift and nobody there knew her well enough to know where she lived. Julia must have called Alfie a dozen times, but he hadn't had any luck either.

Late on Friday night, Dot called to inform Julia that a distant cousin of Gloria's had organised a funeral service at St. Peter's Church after the police released her body. On Saturday morning, exactly one week after Gloria's death during the wedding, Julia made her way down to the church to pay her respects.

Much like on the morning of the wedding, the weather was brutal. The rain lashed down persistently, with icy winds making it impossible to shelter under umbrellas. Julia met Dot and Percy, and they ran to the church, soaked by the time they reached the vestibule.

"A snowstorm *is* coming!" Dot announced as she attempted to fluff up her drowned curls. "The man on the radio said a wall of snow was going to cover the country by the end of the month!"

"Arctic winds," Percy added. "It's going to last until the New Year. They said we were about to enter a mini ice age!"

"They say that every year," Julia assured them. "It's probably just a slow news day."

They sat in one of the back pews, and, as Julia had expected, the church was packed out. She knew it wasn't because of Gloria's popularity. More likely, people were desperate to get a glimpse of whoever had been brought in to replace Father David. It turned out that Father James Cartwright, a vicar from a neighbouring village, had been drafted in for the funeral service. He seemed like a nice man, but he wasn't Father David. Hearing a different voice bellow through the church felt like a betrayal. No one mentioned Father David.

The service was short and sweet, and ended with Gloria's cousin, Iris, an equally large lady of a similar age, giving a short eulogy and thanking everyone for such a great turnout. From her lack of detail, including no mention of the choir Gloria had adored, it was obvious Iris knew very little about the distant cousin she was laying to rest.

Though they were all invited to gather around the grave to say their final goodbyes to Gloria's coffin, very few of the spectators who had come for the gossip value made their way into the graveyard, given the abysmal weather. Julia hadn't intended on sticking around for the whole service, but she couldn't bear the thought of Iris watching her cousin go into the ground without at least a couple of faces of support. With Dot and Percy by her side, they trudged across the waterlogged graveyard with their useless umbrellas plastered to their heads.

When Father James finished the service, Iris stared blankly into the grave as the coffin was slowly lowered to its final resting place. Because of the rain, it was hard to tell if she was crying, but she did wipe her cheeks a couple of times.

The rain finally ceased towards the end of the service, leaving them to toss handfuls of dirt onto the coffin without the rain turning it to mush in their hands. The clouds even parted, allowing the sun to break through.

"Were you friends of Gloria's?" Iris asked as they walked back towards the church.

"Sort of," Julia lied, not wanting to reveal there weren't many people in the village who could have taken such a title. "Were you close with your cousin?"

"Not particularly," Iris explained as they walked into the vestibule. "Truth be told, I hadn't seen her in years. I was shocked to hear about her murder. I was listed as her next of kin, which was a surprise. I guess she didn't really have any other family. I was glad to see so many people in the church. I know she wasn't the most agreeable woman at times, but she had a good heart."

"*Where?*" Dot scoffed, to which Julia elbowed her. "I mean ... *where* are you from?"

"Bourton on Water," Iris replied as she checked her watch, not seeming to notice Dot's indiscretion. "I should get home. My husband will be wondering where I am."

"He doesn't know you're here?" Percy asked.

"There's a reason I haven't seen Gloria in years." Iris sighed. "It doesn't really matter anymore, does it? None of it really matters in the end."

"What happened?" Dot asked a little too eagerly.

"The last time I saw her, I invited her to lunch," Iris started, her eyes clouding over as she appeared to slip into her memories. "I hadn't seen her for a couple of years. We'd get together every so often, if only out of habit. I invited her to my cottage for lunch. Everything was as pleasant as always, but when she left, we noticed an antique clock was missing from our mantelpiece. It was a family heirloom on my husband's side, passed down through the generations. We had it appraised, and they confirmed that it was a genuine piece from the Regency era. The thing was worth a small fortune, but it had sentimental value for my husband. We joked that we'd sell the clock if we were ever short of money, but I always knew we could be homeless and he'd still cling to that thing until his dying breath."

"And Gloria took it?" Dot asked. "I always knew there was something fishy about her!"

"I called Gloria the moment we noticed it was gone, but she denied even seeing a clock on the mantlepiece. As you can imagine, the disappearance of a two-hundred-year-old clock was enough to cut all ties."

"Why would Gloria steal your clock?" Percy asked.

"Well, I don't think she did," Iris continued. "She had brought a friend with her. She never called ahead of time to ask, she just showed up with her. She didn't even introduce us. I had to stretch the food out to four, and the woman ate like she'd never been fed!"

"What did the friend look like?" Julia asked.

"A waiflike woman with straggly hair," Iris explained, indicating the height of a child with her hand. "About this tall. Peculiar woman. Freaky, almost. My husband wanted to call the police, but I convinced him not to. I never liked the thing, personally. I've always been more into Victorian décor. Besides, I didn't want to put Gloria in that awkward position. She seemed quite protective of the tiny woman. I was surprised not to see her here today. I thought I might be able to finally get some answers from her." Iris rechecked her watch. "I really should get going. If I miss the next bus, he's going to start asking questions I'm not in the mood to answer. Thanks again for coming. I know Gloria would have appreciated it, in her own special way."

Iris exited the church, leaving the three of them in the vestibule to digest what she had just said.

"She just described Flora," Percy said, his nose wrinkled. "Odd, don't you think?"

Julia had been so wrapped up thinking about Skye during the service that she hadn't noticed Flora wasn't there to say goodbye to her best, and only, friend.

Dot and Percy departed to go for lunch, leaving Julia to stand alone outside the church; they didn't invite her along. She stared at the Christmas market, which had started to pick up now that the rain had passed. She considered fitting in a spot of Christmas shopping if only to avoid spending the rest of the day back at the cottage desperately searching online for any trace of Skye. Julia looked past the market to her dark café, more grateful than ever to have the business in her life. It had taken a week away to realise how it had become her security blanket when times were tough. Without it, she felt like a ship lacking a sail.

Instead of shopping, she decided she was going to

walk to the post office and buy the ingredients to bake something in her café's kitchen. She hadn't picked up a wooden spoon since she had baked the firework biscuits. As she walked past, she cast one last glance in the direction of Gloria's grave, surprised to see someone there. At first, she thought it might have been the gravedigger filling in the hole, but unless the gravedigger was an attractive, English rose beauty in her late-twenties, she knew she was mistaken.

"Skye," Julia breathed aloud.

Julia hopped over the wall and set off towards the still open grave. Skye was looming over it, wearing a black trench-coat that nipped in at her tiny waist. A bunch of red roses, not unlike the ones that had turned up for Julia's wedding, had been laid next to the hole.

"*Skye!*" Julia called. "Stop right there!"

Skye glanced at Julia before setting off in the opposite direction. Julia ran to catch up, her shoes squelching in the sodden grass as she weaved in and out of the headstones. Skye was calmly walking away, albeit at a brisk pace. Julia closed the gap between them and wrapped her arm around Skye's arm.

"*What* do you *want?*" Skye cried, dragging her arm away from Julia. "Leave me *alone!*"

"I just want to talk to you," Julia replied, taken

aback by Skye's volume. "I know you lied about your alibis."

"Is that why you've had Alfie ringing me nonstop?" Skye snapped. "And why you visited my place of work to ask about me? What's *wrong* with you, woman? Are you that *in love* with Alfie that you can't stand the thought of him being with someone else?"

"In love with *Alfie*?" Julia couldn't help but laugh. "Is that what you think?"

"It's *obvious*!" Skye threw her arms wide. "Why else are you in my face questioning me every chance you get? Alfie told me you were investigating the choir, and I just knew you'd pick on me. Women like you always do."

"Women like me?"

"Jealous ones!" Skye pointed her finger in Julia's face. "You're jealous of me. I get it, you're what, forty? But you're still pretty, *and* you have a fiancé, so just leave Alfie alone. Leave *me* alone, for that matter. I don't want to be any part of your game!"

Julia couldn't believe what she was hearing. She wasn't sure if she wanted to laugh or cry.

"I think you've really misunderstood my relationship with Alfie," Julia said in her calmest voice. "He's my adopted daughter's brother. I know there's less than a decade between us, and yes, I feel protective of him, but like a mother would of a son. I care deeply about his happiness, but I'm not *in love* with him."

Skye appeared to be holding her breath. Her nostrils flared, and her cheeks darkened as she glared at Julia.

"So, why the obsession with me?" Skye asked.

"I know you lied about being in the village on the morning of the wedding. There were cameras in the church to capture my wedding, and I saw the video of you confronting Gloria. I know she slapped you, and that you ran away afterwards. You told me you were trapped in a flood."

"Are you surprised?" Skye exhaled, her body relaxing. "A woman I didn't like slapped me and then she died two hours later. I'm not stupid. I know how that looks and sounds. I didn't think it was important. I came here today to put that to bed and pay my respects."

"And the lie about the cinema?" Julia cocked her head. "Alfie told me the truth. You lied and dragged him into it."

"I was at the cinema." Skye's eyes darted down, and she clasped her hands together. "I was at the cinema with another guy, okay? I panicked when you

223

asked, and I didn't want to admit it in front of Alfie. I like him, but we never said we weren't seeing other people. I was just seeing how things went, and I already had a date planned with a guy from work."

"Oh."

"I can get you the camera footage of me being there if you don't believe me," Skye offered, her edges softening. "I was there all night. I stuck around after the film ended and helped one of the new girls with a stock check."

"I believe you," Julia found herself saying. "I could tell you were lying before, but I don't have that feeling now."

"Thank you." Skye half-smiled. "I can see why you're protective of Alfie. He's a great guy. Things might have worked between us if the circumstances were different."

"Can't it work out now?"

"There's too much going on." Skye shook her head as her bright eyes became shiny from welling tears. "I have a lot going on with work and all this stuff with the murders. I need some time on my own to figure out what I want in life. I have a truckload of debt to pay off, and I'm not going to do it working in a cinema. I racked up the debt at university studying fashion design, and yet I've never tried to chase that dream. Life got in the way, and I got complacent. Maybe now's the right time to give it a shot. I'm still young, and the debt isn't going anywhere for a while, so why not try to be happy while I pay it off?" Leah reached into her trench coat and pulled her purse from her inside pocket. She pulled out a pile of notes. "Can you give this to Alfie? It's only half of what I owe him, but it's all I can afford this month. I'll get the rest to him as soon as I can."

Julia nodded that she would as she pocketed the money, but something white and shiny around Skye's neck caught her eye as she put her purse away. Julia dove forward and ripped open Skye's coat. A glistening pearl necklace hung around her neck.

"Where did you get that?" Julia asked as she ran her fingers along the pearls.

"My aunt gave it to me." Skye glared as she stepped away from Julia. "It was a thank you for getting her back into the choir. It's probably just a cheap piece of costume jewellery, but it's the first thing she's ever bought me."

"It's not costume jewellery," Julia said, her heart pounding in her throat. "That's Rita's necklace. It was taken off her corpse right after she was murdered."

Skye stared at Julia as the words sank in. When

they did, she screamed and scrambled for the back of the necklace. She ripped it off and tossed it into the wet grass. They jumped back as though it was about the explode.

"Are you *serious*?" Skye cried as she rubbed at her neck. "How did she get it?"

"Skye, where does your aunt live?" Julia asked, her voice shaking.

"I-I don't know."

"Isn't it weird that you don't know where your aunt lives?"

"She's always been private," Skye replied, her eyes shifting from the necklace to Julia's eyes. "What are you saying? That my aunt ... that she..."

Skye's voice trailed off, and before Julia could finish the sentence for her, her phone rang in her handbag, startling them both. She fished it out to see that Barker was calling her.

"*Julia!*" he panted down the phone as though he'd just been running. "You need to come home right now. There's someone here I think you'll want to talk to."

Julia didn't press Barker with questions; somehow, she knew exactly who was there. She plucked a handkerchief out of her bag and scooped up the necklace. Leaving Skye standing dumbfounded in the graveyard, Julia sprinted home. When she burst into the hallway, she wasn't the tiniest bit shocked to see Flora sitting in the armchair next to the fire, gobbling down a sandwich with Mowgli curled up in her lap.

"I think it's time to explain yourself," Julia said in between her gasps for air, "don't you, Flora?"

Agatha Frost

14

Flora continued to stare into space as one hand shovelled sandwiches and the other stroked Mowgli. Barker appeared from the kitchen with wet hair and a red face. He had a cup of tea, no doubt containing five sugars, in his hand. He passed it to Flora, and she paused to gulp it down.

"I caught her trying to shove these through the letterbox." Barker reached into his pocket and pulled out two gold wedding bands. "It was lucky I was coming out of the bathroom when I did. I had to chase her halfway down the lane in my bath towel! She's an agile little thing."

Barker tipped the rings into her palm. Julia turned them over with her thumb. The yellow gold caught the light as though calling her to put her ring on. Had it really been a week since that dreadful day?

"Has she said anything?" Julia asked, closing her fingers around the rings.

"She sat herself down and asked if I'd make her some sandwiches." Barker folded his arms and turned to Flora. "Could hardly say no, could I?"

"You did the right thing." Julia patted him on the shoulder. "Can you give us some time?"

Barker nodded and retreated into the dining room. When he closed the door behind him, Julia ventured into the sitting room. Flora looked up out of the corner of her eye, but her attention was firmly on Mowgli. She stroked him from tip to tail, causing wild purrs to vibrate in his throat.

"He likes you," Julia said as she perched on the edge of the couch across from Flora.

"William liked me stroking his tail," Flora said as she ran the fluffy mass through her fingers. "It's their pride and joy."

Julia smiled. She stayed quiet for a couple of minutes, merely watching Flora stroke Mowgli. Knowing what she had to do pained her.

"Thank you for returning these." Julia opened her hand. "We really appreciate you bringing them back to us."

"I didn't want them." Flora shrugged, blinking her eyes repeatedly. "Didn't feel right. They never belonged to me, did they?"

Flora looked at the empty plate as though willing more sandwiches to appear. Julia almost offered to make more, but if she did, she knew they would sit there all night while Flora ate everything in the kitchen.

"Where do you live?" Julia asked, consciously keeping her tone soft. "Where's your home?"

"It's in the woods."

"You live in the woods?"

"My house is in the woods." Flora nodded. "William loved the woods. He'd chase the birds for hours. Never caught one though. He wasn't violent like that. Gloria hated cats, but she loved William."

"You weren't at Gloria's funeral today."

"Didn't want to go." Flora rubbed her nose with the back of her fingerless-gloved hand. "I've said my goodbyes to Gloria. She'll understand. She was the only person who knew where I lived. People called her awful things, but she was kind. She'd bring me bags of food. She was good not to get anything that would go bad because she knew I didn't have a fridge. She even gave me this coat."

Julia stared at the pin-covered coat, which she had noticed was many sizes too big for her tiny frame during Flora's first trip to the cottage.

"Can you show me where you live?" Julia asked.

"Why?"

"Because I'd like to see it."

Flora squinted as she decided her answer. After a minute of consideration, she nodded. Julia stood up and lifted Mowgli off Flora's lap. Flora seemed sad to lose her companion, but she stood up all the same. Julia placed Mowgli on the couch and walked into the hallway, nodding for Flora to follow.

"What about *him*?" Flora nodded at the dining room door. "He chased me."

"He doesn't need to know," Julia responded with a wink. "Our little secret."

Flora grinned the first genuine smile Julia had seen from her. Several of her teeth were missing, a true statement to her age, despite her childlike personality.

They set off along the winding path into the village.

Julia knew Flora could run away at any moment if she wanted to, but Julia had a feeling she didn't want to. It felt like they were on a treasure hunt, and Flora was leading them to the jackpot.

They walked around the village green, ignoring the bustling Christmas market. They bypassed the church and set off down the lane to the school. Halfway down the lane, Flora scrambled over the stone wall and waved for Julia to follow. They crossed the field and passed the spot where the bonfire had burned only days ago. Flora walked right through the black patch of charred grass where the fire had roared. Barker had been right; she was a nimble little thing. Julia almost had to jog to keep up with her speedy pace.

They entered Haworth Forest at the exact spot they had talked on the night of the bonfire. Julia suddenly realised where Flora had flitted off to when her back was turned.

Flora manoeuvred through the forest as though she was at one with the space. She hopped over fallen trees and ducked under low-hanging branches without looking. Julia tried her best to follow in her footsteps, but twigs and thorns scratched at her skin.

They walked for what felt a lifetime, until Julia began to wonder if Flora was leading her on a fool's errand. She knew Haworth Forest was dense and spanned several miles, but it had to end eventually.

"Where are we going?" Julia called after Flora, who was way ahead.

Instead of replying verbally, Flora gestured for Julia to follow. Finally, the old woman slowed down. They walked for another minute before reaching a steep, muddy hill. At the top of the hill, Julia looked down at a rundown cottage. It had bricks missing from the walls, and parts of the roof were absent. Julia wondered if Flora was playing a trick on her, but the sprightly woman set off down the slope, bouncing from tree to tree. Julia attempted to copy her route, but she slipped several times, muddying her jeans in the process. When she reached the bottom of the slope, Flora had already withdrawn into the cottage.

As Julia crept towards the strange building, she suddenly remembered a story from her youth. Children at school had talked about a witch who lived in the forest in her own house, not unlike the lady from the Hansel and Gretel fairy tale. The children would scare each other by telling wild stories about the things she did to anyone who dared venture inside. Julia had always known it was nothing more than a tale, but it had kept her from exploring too far into the dense wood. It struck her that this was the furthest she had travelled, despite being born and raised in the village. Was Flora the witch from the story? All the best tales had an element of truth in them, after all.

Casting those silly thoughts from her mind, Julia walked towards the front door. It was inches shy of the ground and looked like it might rot off any second. She pushed on it, and its hinges screamed out for oil. What met Julia inside made her jaw drop.

Flora sat in an old rocking chair in the corner under a hole in the roof. Light streamed through, but a plastic sheet had been hung to protect the indoors from the elements. The glassless windows were boarded with wood, and leaves provided a carpet underfoot. A metal-framed bed topped with a thin mattress and scratchy-looking sheets stood near a portable fireplace that seemed to run on gas canisters.

It wasn't the furniture that commanded Julia's attention, however; it was the overwhelming number of items on display. She didn't know where to cast her eyes first. An upturned milk crate was adorned with dozens of glass ornaments; another was topped with as many ticking clocks. Trinkets of gold and silver glistening in the light lined a shelving unit. Julia took a step in, wanting to see more.

Jewellery boxes of all shapes and sizes sat on the window ledge, each stuffed with handfuls of jewellery. There were even three bicycles, a pile of shoes, jars of buttons, and an empty pram. Some items looked worthless, while others looked like they held extreme value. A small clock sat with pride of place on another window ledge, and even though Julia wasn't an expert when it came to style, she would have bet her life that it dated back to the Regency era.

"What is all this stuff?"

"My treasures," Flora explained, her tone hinting that it should have been obvious.

"Did you steal all of this stuff?" Julia asked. "Flora, this is unbelievable."

"It's not stealing!" Flora snapped, her head shaking. "It's *taking*. It's different. I can't help it. I see things, and I know I have to have them, and it doesn't stop until I do."

"What doesn't stop?"

"The *feeling*." She stamped her finger on her chest. "The compulsion. I've had it since I was a little girl. My mother called the feeling 'the magpie' inside of me. I'd take her things and hide them. I didn't know why; it just made me feel good. It's like they speak to me. They *want* me to have them."

Julia was at a loss for words. She had never seen such a vast array of different items under one roof.

"And nobody knows you live here?" Julia asked. "People must walk out here."

"Nobody ever does." Flora shook her head. "Only Gloria knew, and now you do. It's nobody's business."

"Do you have any power?" Julia asked, stepping further into the cluttered space. "Or water?"

Flora shook her head.

"How do you eat?"

"People feed me." Flora kicked her feet off the edge of the rocking chair; they barely scraped the ground. "Gloria always made sure I ate when she saw me. And she brought me gas for the fire. She was a good woman. She looked after me."

"Why do you have to live like this?" Julia crept forward and sat on the edge of the bed. It cried out under her weight, and the mattress felt damp to the core. "Surely the council could help you. What about your pension?"

"Never claimed it." Flora shrugged. "They kept trying to put me in places. They never wanted to help me, they just wanted to put me away. Timothy, my brother, wanted to put me away. He called me a 'problem'. They kept sticking labels on me, saying I had 'this' and 'that'. I knew it was all just a way to keep me being 'Freaky Flora', so I turned my back on them. I found this place, and I knew nobody lived here. I kept coming back and watching, but no one ever passed by."

Julia's heart broke for Flora. She was sure one of those labels had been 'kleptomaniac', but she didn't want to push Flora over the edge, so she bit her tongue.

"Did you take the church items?" Julia asked calmly.

Flora nodded, her eyes dropping to the floor.

"Why?"

"They were my biggest treasures," Flora said, a smile flicking momentarily across her lips. "They spoke to me for years, but I never touched them. I knew they were forbidden. They were the only items I'd ever resisted. It was a way of knowing that I was still okay. I still had control of the feeling. But then William died, and I lost control. When I woke up on the morning of your wedding, I knew I had to have them. They told me to stop resisting."

"And Rita caught you."

"She thought I was going to sell them!" Flora cried, casting her eyes around her home. "Why would I *sell* my treasures? They're worth more than money."

Julia joined Flora in looking around. She wanted to

see things through her eyes, but it was a difficult task. She wondered if Flora recognised the irony of living in such extreme poverty while also being surrounded by items worth a fortune.

"Rita blackmailed me," Flora continued, looking at Julia for the first time since they had ventured into the woods. "She demanded that I sell the stuff I took and give her half the money. When I refused, she said she'd call the police. I didn't know what to do. I panicked."

"So, you tried to poison her?" Julia prompted. "With arsenic?"

"I took it from a museum," Flora explained. "Years ago. I didn't think it was even real. I just wanted to teach her a lesson, so I sprinkled a few bits into her water when she was in the bathroom in the pub. People have never paid me any attention. I move around this village unseen. People always look the other way. It's made it easy to find my treasures."

"A few drops are all it takes," Julia said with a sigh. "It's extremely toxic to human beings."

"I know that now." Flora sniffled and wiped her nose. Tears flowed freely down her mucky cheeks. "I didn't know what to do when Gloria took Rita's water bottle. That wasn't how it was supposed to happen. I tried to tell her, but she was getting in the zone for the performance. She batted me away and wouldn't listen. She kept drinking it for her throat. When nothing happened, I thought it'd been a prop. I thought everything was going to be okay."

"But then the coughing started."

"I *tried* to warn her!" Flora sobbed. "She wouldn't listen. She *never* listened."

"Why did you come to see me?" Julia asked. "If you were behind Gloria's death, why did you ask me to find the culprit?"

"Because they said you were the best!" Flora's eyes looked deep into Julia's. "They said you'd get to the bottom of it. I thought if you looked, you might find another reason that she died. Or, maybe, you'd figure out what Rita was doing to me, and you'd help. I was confused."

Flora paused and inhaled. Rain began falling again, pattering on the plastic sheet covering the hole.

"Rita must have known it was you who killed Gloria," Julia said. "What happened next?"

"She got worse!" Flora cried. "She kept telling me to sell the items or she'd tell everyone what I did. She didn't even care that Gloria was dead. She thanked me. It was finally her time to take control. When she kicked me out of the choir in front of everyone, it was her way of sending me a message. But I wasn't going to sell them! I couldn't. They meant too much."

"So, you stabbed Rita?"

"I didn't want to." Flora inhaled deeply. "I went to talk to her. I thought if I explained that they were my treasures, she'd understand I couldn't sell them. She didn't understand. She laughed at me. She called me 'Freaky Flora' over and over. It was like a chant. We were in the kitchen. I picked up a knife off the counter, and I pointed at her. She soon changed her tune. She backed away with her hands up. Part of me liked seeing her like that. She begged for her life, but I knew I'd gone too far. I needed to make it all stop. It was so easy. The knife just went in, and that was it. She dropped to the floor, and I ran."

"Not before taking her jewellery," Julia added softly. "They were Rita's treasures."

"She didn't *deserve* them!" Flora spat. "A woman like that doesn't deserve any nice things. I'd always known those pearls belonged to me, I'd just never had the opportunity before."

Julia reached into her handbag and pulled out the pearls in their handkerchief. Flora's eyes lit up.

"Why did you give them to Skye if they meant that much to you?"

"Skye was nice to me." Flora smiled again. "I kept my distance because I knew her father had infected my name, but when it mattered, she was nice to me. She let me back into the choir. I shared them with her because I knew she'd treasure them as much as I did."

Julia put the pearls away. She didn't have the heart to tell Flora that Skye thought they were a cheap piece of costume jewellery.

"And Father David?" Julia prompted. "Why did you frame him?"

"I wanted all of this to go away," Flora muttered, her eyes drifting down to her lap. "I thought killing Rita would make things stop, but I could feel the police closing in. I'm ashamed of what I did to him. I overheard him talking on the phone about owing money weeks ago. I knew I needed to give back the church treasures. They'd caused so much trouble. I didn't want them anymore. I knew I should never have taken them, so I returned them."

"With the arsenic, and a letter pushing the police to search his vestry."

"I told you, I'm *ashamed* of that." Flora wiped away more tears. "Father David is a good man. He was kind to me, but I did what I had to do. I regretted it the second I heard he'd been arrested, but it was too late.

That's why I was returning your rings to you. You'd been so kind to me, so I knew they didn't belong to me. I wanted to do something right."

Julia was grateful to have her rings back, but she didn't like what had to come next. They sat in a comfortable silence as the minutes passed by. As Flora rocked back and forth in her chair, Julia hoped she was coming to terms with the consequences of her actions.

"You know you have to tell the truth to the police?" Julia explained gently, breaking the silence. "You need to tell them what you just told me, or Father David will suffer for what you did. They've already charged him, and that's not fair, is it?"

Flora shook her head.

"What's going to happen to me?" Flora asked in the timid voice of a child.

"I don't know," Julia admitted. "I honestly don't know, but I hope they give you the help you need."

They sat in silence again until the rain finally stopped. When it did, the clouds cleared, and the bright sun broke through the trees. It shone down on Flora through the gap in the roof. She leaned back in her chair and tilted her face up to the sunlight, a smile on her face. Julia let her sit there until the sun hid again. When it did, she stood up and walked over to the door.

She opened it and waited for Flora to follow.

"I think I might have a problem," Flora mumbled faintly as she climbed off the rocking chair. "Gloria was right. She was always right. She'd think this whole thing was so silly." Flora shuffled to the door and looked up at Julia. "Will you come with me?"

"Of course."

Flora reached into her pocket and pulled out a silver locket. Julia grabbed at her neck and realised the locket Jessie had given her to celebrate a year of being together wasn't around her neck. She cast her mind back, but she couldn't remember when she had last worn it; things had been so hectic.

"I found it down the side of your chair." Flora explained as she dropped the locket into Julia's hand. "All the best treasures are down there, you just need to remember to look."

Julia accepted the locket and fastened it back around her neck. They climbed back up the muddy slope and set off through Haworth Forest. They walked in silence towards Flora's fate. Julia had no idea what Flora was thinking about, but Julia was praying that the powers in charge of Flora's fate treated her with some compassion.

15

Christmas Day

For the first time in her life, Julia spent Christmas morning at church. She sat at the back of the congregation and joined in with the hymns she knew. It was a cathartic and blissful experience, and by the end of the service, she was glad she had attended. She was also glad to be in attendance for Father David's return as official vicar of St. Peter's

Church.

As people filed out of the church in an orderly line, Julia joined Father David at the front, where he was busy gathering his papers.

"Merry Christmas, Father."

"And Merry Christmas to you, Julia!" He beamed from the pulpit. "I can't tell you how happy I was to look out and see your face. I owe you my life."

"I did what anyone would have done."

"I'm not so sure." His smile softened, and his eyes drifted away. "But thank God you saw the light. Thank God, indeed."

"Did you enjoy your break?"

"I did!" Father David clapped his hands together. "After my official pardon and the apology from the police, some rest and recuperation were exactly what I needed! The Church was kind enough to allow me some time off, and I heard Father James did a splendid job in my absence. I spent a jubilant month on a beach in Lanzarote! I never thought I'd enjoy such a trip, but do you know what I realised while I was locked up for those few days? I realised I'd never had a holiday at the beach! I'd always go to cities, or to stays with friends in Wales. Contemplating a future behind bars made me re-evaluate life. I vowed to God that if I were given a second chance at freedom, I wouldn't waste a second of it."

"It sounds like you had a great time."

"I'm glad to be back!" he announced. "Back in my home and back in my church. And what better day to return than on the day of Jesus' birth? A day of hope, renewal, and fresh beginnings. You can almost taste it in the air, can't you?"

"I can." Julia smiled, affected by Father David's new zest for life. "Have you heard anything about Flora?"

"Ah, poor Flora." He pulled off his glasses and rubbed them on the edge of his robe. "I must admit, it pains me to know she's taken my place. I've been allowed to visit her numerous times, and she seems to be in high spirits!"

"Do you know what's going to happen to her?"

"They're evaluating her as we speak," he said as he perched his glasses back on his nose. "I pray the judge sends her to a hospital instead of a prison. It's her only chance of salvation from her demons. I spoke to her lawyer, and he's hopeful the result will swing her way. I've volunteered to be a character witness to show that I've forgiven her transgressions."

"I'm praying too," Julia admitted, a little

sheepishly. "I don't know who to. God, an energy, the clouds. I feel like I need to do something."

"And I'm sure whoever you're praying to is receiving loud and clear." He offered her a warming smile. "Have faith, my dear. You're a good woman. In fact, you're so good, you've been stood in front of me for five minutes, and you've yet to ask me why I owed so much money."

"I wasn't going to."

"Then you're the only person in the village who won't." He chuckled before inhaling. "But I feel I must be honest. I have a younger brother, Harold. Like Flora, Harold has had a troubled life. I've tried to bring him into the light many times, but my help always falls on deaf ears. Still, I keep trying, as God would want me to. Harold fell into online gambling a while back, and it's been getting worse and worse every year. He wrote me a gut-wrenching letter begging for my help. I knew it wouldn't fix the problem, but I couldn't turn away when my flesh and blood was crying out. I called the company he owed the money to, and I paid it off using my savings. I'm not a rich man, but I'm frugal, so I had a nice nest egg. I'm afraid that after paying his debt and taking my month-long holiday I don't have much left, but I'm at peace with that. I have air in my lungs, and

I'm able to walk around as a free man. Not everyone can say that."

"It's really good to have you back, Father."

"It's good to be back!" He looked around the church and grinned. "I have a feeling everything is going to be all right. Are you still wanting to do that thing you asked of me?"

"Only if you can."

"Everything is in place." He gathered his things and set off towards the vestry. "I think it's about time, don't you? See you at two!"

***

Julia left the church and returned to Dot's cottage, where the entire family were gathered for Christmas lunch.

"There you are!" Dot cried, oven gloves covering her hands. "I was about to send out a search party. You said you were going for some fresh air. Where did you go? To the Himalayas and back?"

"Something like that."

"Well, you're just in time," Julia's father called from the kitchen. "Turkey's almost done!"

"Ugh, I'm starving," Jessie wailed.

"You haven't stopped eating all day," Barker reminded her, prodding her in the stomach. "I didn't even get a look in on that box of chocolates."

"It's Christmas!" she cried. "Don't hate the player, hate the game."

"At least share, sis." Alfie swiped at the box of chocolates cradled on Jessie's lap. "You've eaten all the good ones!"

Julia collapsed on the sofa next to Barker and snuggled into his side. She gave him a thumbs up to let him know the plan was still going ahead. He kissed the top of her head, and they turned to the TV and watched a re-run of a classic Christmas episode of *The Royle Family*.

When Brian announced that lunch was served, they all crammed around Dot's tiny dining room table. Sue and Neil's twins, Pearl and Dottie, who had been born on this very day one whole year ago, had birthday hats and badges on, but everyone else wore Christmas hats and knitted jumpers except for Julia, who wore a simple, white, comfortable dress.

They stuffed themselves with the delicious Christmas dinner Dot and Brian had spent the whole morning arguing over. When they were finished, Dot immediately brought out the giant Christmas pudding

Julia had made. She placed it in the middle of the table and poured a whole pan of boiling hot brandy on top. Before Julia could say anything, Dot lit the pudding with a match, and a giant fireball flew up from the cake, lighting the hanging decorations on fire.

"Two to three *tablespoons*, Gran!" Julia cried as she wafted the smoke.

"Well, I didn't know!" Dot cried, shaking the pan in the air as she stormed off into the kitchen. "Maybe you should have written it down some—*oh*, you did! My mistake, dear!

The flaming Christmas pudding burned like a campfire in the middle of the table. Julia should have been disappointed that her creation had been ruined, but it was just another Dot moment to add to the memory bank for later laughter.

As they tucked into mince pies instead, the front door opened, bringing in a gust of cold air.

"*Ho, ho, ho!*" Percy announced, walking into the dining room dressed in a Santa Claus outfit, complete with a giant sack. "Merry Christmas, one and all!"

Pearl and Dottie's faces lit up at Santa's arrival, but Vinnie threw his head back and wailed. Katie bounced him up and down on her knee while Percy laughed and rubbed his fake belly.

"I come bearing gifts!" He shook the red sack. "Take one and pass it along. They're all the same, so don't be picky."

Julia took the sack first and passed it down to Barker. She waited until they all had a matching oblong, wrapped box before ripping back the paper.

"A VHS of my famous performance at the Cheltenham Playhouse Theatre!" he announced. "Recorded in 1987!"

"Percy," Julia said as she turned the outdated videotape over in her hands. "You shouldn't have."

"How do we even play this?" Jessie whispered to Barker.

"We don't," Barker whispered back. "Just say thank you and never bring it up again."

"Thanks." Jessie waved it over her head. "Love it."

"No-*ho-ho-ho* problem, young one!" Percy patted his stomach, chuckling at his own joke. "Where's my Dorothy at?"

"Hanging her head in shame for turning the Christmas pudding into a meteor," Julia said, leaning on her chair to investigate the kitchen. "Gran? Percy's here?"

"*Percy?*" Dot hurried out of the kitchen, a smile on her face. "Oh, you made it!"

"I wouldn't have missed it for the world, my dear." Percy leaned in and kissed her on the cheek. "You look divine. Christmas suits you."

"Oh, thank you," Dot pulled at her jumper. "I knitted it myself."

"*Liar!*" Jessie coughed under her breath. "You couldn't knit a sock for a cat."

"Well, I thought about knitting it," Dot said with pursed lips, "but I realised my time was better spent giving to charity."

"When have you ever given to charity?" Barker asked.

"You're all here, aren't you?" Dot fired back with an icy glare. "Eating my food under my roof. Yes, I thought so."

"Well, either way, you look as beautiful as always." Percy gave her another kiss on the cheek. "Are you ready for your Christmas gift, Dorothy?"

"You got me something?" Dot pushed up her curls at the back.

"Of course!" Percy announced with a flourish. "How could I not get the most beautiful woman in the whole village a gift befitting her? Are you ready?"

Dot nodded and looked at the sack on the floor, but it was empty. Percy started clicking behind Dot's ears, producing silver coins and then making them disappear.

"Wait, has he been practising?" Barker whispered to Julia. "That's actually quite good."

Julia was equally impressed by Percy's sudden showmanship. She watched as the coins disappeared and reappeared, wondering how he was performing the trick. At the moment when Dot seemed to be growing tired with the clicking next to her ears, Percy clicked one final time, producing a diamond ring.

"What is happening right now?" Sue squealed, half standing up in her chair.

"Dorothy South." Percy dropped to one knee, his tone serious and steady. "These past two months with you have been the happiest of my life. I know this is sudden, and I know it probably seems a bit silly at our age, but hell, if everyone else can do it, why can't we? Throw caution to the wind, I say. We might not have long left, but I know I want to spend however many days I have right by your side. I can't promise you a lifetime because I don't have one left, but I can promise you the rest of my life. Dorothy South, I love you. What do you say? Will you be my wife?"

Julia's hand clasped over her mouth as she stared at her gran. All the air sucked from the room, and not a sound could be heard. Dot appeared frozen in time, her mouth agape as she stared at the ring.

"Yes," Dot said finally, followed by a small girlish laugh. "Yes, I'll marry you."

It was Jessie of all people who jumped up and started clapping. Julia couldn't help but join. Tears streamed down her face as she watched Percy slide the shiny ring onto Dot's wrinkled finger. Julia turned to Sue, who was sobbing into a Christmas napkin. Even Brian and Katie were shedding tears.

"Did I just dream that?" Barker hooked his thumb over his shoulder.

"I don't think you did." Julia shook her head. "My eighty-four-year-old grandmother is getting married."

"All right, Percy," Dot ordered. "You can get up. I said yes!"

"I don't think I can, dear." He waved his hands. "I appear to be stuck down here. Old bones, you see!"

Alfie and Barker jumped up and hoisted Percy to his feet. When he was upright again, he caught his balance and produced a piece of mistletoe from thin air. He held it above his fiancée's head, and they shared a kiss.

"*To Gran and Percy!*" Sue held her glass of buck's fizz in the air. "And I thought we couldn't top last

Christmas with the twins coming and Barker proposing to Julia, but here we are, an octogenarian engagement! Now *that* is something you don't see every day."

"And I have more good news!" Percy announced. "The remnants of the Peridale Harmonics Choir met last night, and they voted for me to be the new leader! My first job is to recruit some new members, so what do you say, folks? Are you all on board?"

"Actually, Percy, I think I'm going to have to quit." Alfie rose his hand in the air. "The whole experience left a bad taste in my mouth."

"Me too, dear," Dot said as she stared at her glittering ring. "I'll happily cheer you on from the sidelines as your wife, but I think my singing days are well behind me!"

"What about your *Miss Singing Peridale 1953* title?" Julia asked. "Would *she* ever stop singing?"

"About that." Dot pushed up her curls as her eyelids fluttered. "I *may* have won that by default because there were only two entrants and the other girl wet herself on stage and ran off before finishing her song."

"Gran…" Sue sighed. "You were so proud of that title."

"I still won the money, dear!" Dot announced.

"'Don't cry for me, Argentina!'"

Julia sipped her buck's fizz and choked when she noticed it was only a couple of minutes to two.

"Everyone up!" she announced after slapping the table. "The excitement isn't over yet. We all need to get across to the church right now!"

"The church?" Dot sighed. "I've spent enough time in there lately. You're not making us sit through one of those boring Christmas services, are you?"

"No," Julia said, grabbing Barker's hand. "We're getting married."

"*Married*?" Sue cried. "But—but—the dress, the flowers, the reception—I'm wearing a Christmas jumper! What are you talking about?"

"We don't need any of that stuff," Julia said as she looked into Barker's eyes. "All that matters is that there's a man who wants to marry a woman and woman who wants to marry a man. What's more fitting than marrying on the one-year anniversary of our engagement? Now, chop-chop everyone! Father David is waiting."

"Let me grab my hat!" Dot announced.

"Leave it!" Julia cried, grabbing her gran's hand. "We're all going as we are, and that includes you, Santa."

Julia and Barker led the way across the village green to the church. Dot and Percy's promised snowstorm had yet to hit the country, but the weather was cold enough to chill Julia, wearing only the simple dress she had dug out of her wardrobe. She had considered bringing her wedding dress with her. Jessie had secretly had it dry cleaned, but it felt wrong to repeat the occasion in that dress. That was then, and this was now, and she finally understood what a wedding was about: the marriage of two people.

"We thought you'd chickened out!" Roxy exclaimed, shivering in the vestibule with Johnny and Leah. "Come on, bride! Let's get this over with before the fat lady sings again."

Without pomp or extravagance, they made their way down the aisle in one collective group. Halfway down, Julia's father looped his arm through hers. She smiled up at him, feeling worlds apart from how she'd felt the first time. The quivering, nervous wreck of a bride had been replaced with a determined and confident woman about to marry the man she loved.

"Ah, here you are!" Father David clapped his hands together when he saw them. "Is everyone here?"

Julia looked around the church. She had her family and her friends right by her side. She looked down at her pearl engagement ring, and then up at the ceiling. She knew her mother was there too.

"Everyone that matters," Julia said. "Let's do this."

Father David grinned throughout the entire service. Tears flowed freely as Julia and Barker exchanged vows. Julia cried too, but they were more tears of relief that her wedding was finally happening for real.

"I now pronounce you husband and wife!" Father David cried, his voice bellowing around the empty church. "You can now kiss the bride."

As Julia and Barker shared their first kiss as a married couple, applause to rival a stadium full of people filled the room. A weight vanished from Julia's shoulders, and when she opened her eyes, she smiled wider than she ever had, glad she wasn't dreaming.

"Any regrets?" Barker whispered.

"Not one," Julia replied, her fingers locked behind his head. "Now give me another kiss, husband."

After signing the marriage certificate, everyone insisted on taking pictures on their phones to immortalise the moment. Once they'd posed in various groups, Julia and Barker walked down the aisle hand in hand as husband and wife. They walked through the front doors, and Julia gasped when she saw soft flakes of snow drifting from the pale sky.

"Would you look at that," Dot said. "Someone is looking down on you, Julia."

"Thanks, Mum," Julia whispered to the sky.

They stood in the snow for a moment and let the first flakes of the year powder their hair.

"What now?" Jessie asked.

"We go back and enjoy Christmas," Julia said, squeezing Barker's hand. "What do you say, husband?"

"Sounds like a plan to me, wife."

And with that, they all trekked back to Dot's cottage to spend the rest of the day in front of the television with great food and even better company— the only way Christmas should be spent.

THANK YOU FOR READING &
DON'T FORGET TO REVIEW!

I hope you all enjoyed venturing into Peridale once again!

If you did enjoy the book, **please consider** writing a review. They help us reach more people! I appreciate any feedback, no matter how long or short. It's a great way of letting other cozy mystery fans know what you thought about the book.

Being an independent author means this is my livelihood, and every review really does make a huge difference. Reviews are the best way to support me so I can continue doing what I love, which is bringing you, the readers, more fun adventures in Peridale! Thank you for spending time in Peridale, and I hope to see you again soon!

ALSO BY AGATHA FROST

If you enjoyed *Wedding Cake and Woes*, why not sign up to Agatha Frost's **FREE** newsletter at **AgathaFrost.com** to hear about brand new releases!

You can also find Agatha on **FACEBOOK**, **TWITTER**, and **INSTAGRAM**. Simply search '**Agatha Frost**'.

The 16th book in the Peridale Café series is coming early 2019! Julia and friends will be back for another Peridale Cafe Mystery case soon.

34942329R00163

Made in the USA
Lexington, KY
29 March 2019